Advance praise for *E*

"Wynant Vanderpoel has used Dostoevsky's 'The Grand Inquisitor' as the starting point for a contemporary spiritual exploration of faith and doubt. He has written a fascinating and daring literary fable. Anyone concerned with how to live in the disenchanted world in which we now find ourselves will want to read this book."

– Lee Patterson, F.W. Hilles Professor of English, Emeritus, Yale University

"The author has taken an old and venerable tale of faith from Dostoevsky and injected it into the modern world of Sam Harris and Richard Dawkins. Be warned: he is persuasive."

– Samuel Sachs, Director Emeritus, The Frick Collection

"This story undertakes the imaginative challenge of interweaving elements of a great Russian novel with a fast-paced generational tale to set forth questions about modern faith and morality. You can't help but be moved."

– John Wilmerding, Professor of American Art, Emeritus, Princeton University

"Very interesting, entertaining and relevant."

– Russell Banks, Author

Enigma

A Literary Fable

by

Wynant D. Vanderpoel

Library of Congress Control Number: 2010906088
ISBN: Hardcover 978-1-4500-9152-7
Softcover 978-1-4500-9151-0
Ebook 978-1-4500-9153-4

First Edition

Designed by the Vanderpoel Group
Wynant D. Vanderpoel and Holley Flagg

This book was printed in the United States of America.

To order additional copies of this book, contact:
Xlibris Corporation
1-888-795-4274
www.Xlibris.com
Orders@Xlibris.com
72905

About the Type

Enigma: A Literary Fable was set in Bembo. Based on a typeface cut by Francesco Griffo in 1495, Bembo was first used for the Italian Cardinal Pietro Bembo's short text, *De Aetna*. The typeface that we see today, designed in 1929, is a revival by Stanley Morison for the Monotype Corporation in London of that old-style Roman typeface and other typefaces that had been lost for centuries. The Lanston Monotype Company of Philadelphia brought Bembo to the United States in the 1930s. The well-proportioned letter forms are quiet and simple, providing unusual legibility and a timeless, classical character.

In memory of

Hannah Locke Carter
and
Malcolm Evans McAlpin

Special thanks to

Edmund Keeley
my undergraduate creative writing professor
presently professor emeritus of English
Princeton University

Madeleine Findlay
publisher
Single Island Press

Introduction

While at an Episcopal boarding school during the 1950s, I was introduced to Fyodor Dostoevsky's novel *The Brothers Karamazov*. The school required students to take a sacred studies course each year, and no doubt Dostoevsky's masterpiece was assigned reading as the main characters all wrestle with the question of God's existence.

Book 5, chapter 5 of the novel, known as "The Grand Inquisitor," once read and digested, stays with you. At least with me it did. Over the years, now and again, "The Grand Inquisitor" would pop up on my cortex radar screen, and I would remind myself to refresh my memory and reread it.

Fifty years passed before I did so; then one day I was browsing in a bookstore, and there before me was a thin paperback entitled *Notes from the Underground / The Grand Inquisitor*. I purchased a copy and, over the following weeks, read it a number of times, drawing fresh insights with each reading. If the reader is unfamiliar with "The Grand Inquisitor," a brief story line will be useful, although I encourage reading the aforementioned chapter directly, for what I have written plays off it.

In brief, two Karamazov brothers meet. Ivan has composed a poem he wishes to read to his younger brother, Alyosha. The setting is Seville, Spain, in the sixteenth century during the worst time of the Spanish Inquisition. The cardinal, who, the day before, had burned nearly one hundred heretics in a grand auto-da-fé, passes by the Seville cathedral to see Christ healing a blind man and then raising a young child who has died. Quickly, the cardinal has his guards seize Christ and take Him to the palace dungeon. That evening the cardinal visits Christ and shares his thoughts with Him. And what thoughts he shares! Christ does not speak, for He cannot—as it is written—until Judgment Day.

When the cardinal has finished speaking, he gives Him a choice: He can go free if He will return from whence He came, or if He is going to hang around and stir up trouble, the cardinal will burn Him at the stake the following morning. Christ kisses the cardinal on his lips and goes free.

What occurred to me and prompts what follows was how Christ might be questioned in the twenty-first century.

Enigma: A Literary Fable is simply a spiritual inquiry, but it is one that hopes to encourage the reader to consider his or her own thinking about religion, a subject that is arguably more timely than ever, with Christianity and Islam on the edge of, if not actually in, a holy war, with each claiming God on its side.

Yet with the woes of sin and strife the world has suffered long/ Beneath the heavenly hymn have rolled two thousand years of wrong/ And warring human kin hears not the tidings which they bring.

—the hymn "It Came upon a Midnight Clear"
(Lyrics: Edmund Sears / Music: Richard Willis)

Didn't you tell me that if it were mathematically proved to you that truth was outside Christ, you would rather remain with Christ than with truth?

—Fyodor Dostoevsky, *The Devils*

If a man extols his own faith and disparages another because he wants to glorify it, he seriously injures his own faith.

—third-century BCE Indian emperor, Ashoka

h, Alyosha, as I promised, I have come for one more talk with you as I said I might. But first you must accept my apologies in my delay, for I am a bit past my thirtieth birthday, but that is beside the point.”

“Once again you surprise me, Ivan. How time flies! And, dear brother, I have not forgotten your promise. To think we meet again certainly gives pause for thought. But tell me, what is on your mind to share with me this day?”

“Alyosha,” Ivan laughed, “you no doubt remember that poem in prose, ‘The Grand Inquisitor,’ I had you listen to?”

“But of course. How could I forget?”

“Well, I have had a few years—one hundred and thirty-one to be precise—to ruminate on my ridiculous thing, as I described it. And when I knew we were to meet, I was inspired to write another version, a modern version.”

“A modern version, eh?”

“Well, you must admit, Alyosha, what I wrote in 1879 is a bit dated now.”

“But your piece was so original, Ivan, so clever, although I never told you so.”

“Your Karamazov blood still runs strong,” Ivan beamed, “but enough of your brotherly affection. Again, you will be my first listener if you will so indulge me, Alyosha?”

"Ivan, as with the first time, I am all attention."

"So be it. This modern version I call 'Enigma: A Literary Fable.' It takes place not in sixteenth century Seville, Spain, but in America, in the heart of the Adirondack Mountains at the beginning of the twenty-first century in a fictitious hamlet I call Dixville Crossing."

"Ah, America!"

"Yes, Alyosha, America, where Dmitri and Grushenka fled to escape the mines in Siberia. That was the plan, you remember. They settled on some land in the Adirondack Mountains and tilled the soil for ten years, not the three they had planned on staying. You see, it took them longer to learn the English, and besides, Grushenka loved America. The land was raw and rugged indeed, filled with wild bears and big cats, too. The redskins, however, were not very much in evidence, and they never did lay eyes on a Mohican. But a frontier land it was, and that was what they went in search of."

"But today, in the twenty-first century, Ivan, do these Adirondacks still look the way they did when Dmitri and Grushenka were there?"

"Surprisingly, they do, Alyosha. Surprisingly, they do, which is why I set my modern version there and to rekindle my fond memories when I visited them. But let me begin."

The last time the valley had so much snow was back in '92. Thirty-two inches had fallen over the last two and a half days. But this was only late October, not March, when heavy, late snowfalls are not uncommon. Leaves still clung to the trees, although fall colors had long since passed. The final flakes descended early Sunday morning, with daylight saving time officially ending the night before. Quietly but quickly, low pressure took leave of the valley, ushering in colder temperatures with winds swirling, causing the snow to come cascading through the trees, especially the towering white pines, making it seem as if the storm had not left at all.

Normally, it took Thomas a quarter of an hour to walk into town, but anticipating that the road had not been plowed since yesterday evening, he allowed twice the time. Too, his legs weren't what they used to be. He'd had a couple of falls recently, and if Dana were still alive, she wouldn't have thought of letting him walk to church with all the fresh snow. There must have been a foot of it on the road as he set out with Molly, his six-year-old yellow Lab, and nary a sign that any vehicle had passed. In fact, it took Thomas and Molly thirty-five minutes to reach the First Congregational Church on Main Street. He had to stop several times to catch his breath, even though the walk was downhill. In his mid-eighties now, it didn't take too much activity to get his heart pounding. Although a number of homes were along his route, he saw no one else. Odd, he thought, no one out shoveling. Watching the two of them was a study in contrasts, Thomas moving slowly but steadily, Molly romping with abandon.

The path from Main Street to the church was not cleared either, and there were no footprints in the snow to indicate others had preceded Thomas. The six steps leading up to the entrance of the church were barely defined because of the snowfall. Thomas felt his way tentatively. Halfway, he slipped and fell forward, striking his head, near his right temple, on the top step. "Damn," he muttered. Stars flashed across his eyes. Molly rushed to his side and dutifully began licking his face encouragingly. "OK, girl, I'm OK." He took a minute to gather himself before slowly rising to his feet and brushing himself free of the snow he had collected. Even more carefully, he negotiated the remaining steps and entered the church, took his parka off, and hung it on a peg in the vestibule. Then he brushed off Molly's feet. Since Dana's passing, Ralph Hardin, the pastor, had let Thomas bring Molly into the vestibule on Sundays and had provided a cushion under the coat rack, where Molly would curl up, greet the congregation with her thumping tail, and nap off and on until the service concluded. Once Thomas settled Molly on the cushion, he entered through a second set of doors to the church proper. No one was inside. Two candles were lit at either side of the communion table, an unadorned cross affixed above and between them. Thomas walked partway down the center aisle that split ten rows of pews, selected a pew on his left, sat down close to the aisle, and bowed his head in prayer, although his usual thoughts were not as focused because of the oddity of his singular presence just before the eleven o'clock service. The First Congregational Church was modest as churches go, seating two hundred or so at capacity; from where Thomas sat, the raised platform with the pulpit to the left and the lectern to the right was but twenty feet away.

When he lifted his head from prayers, seated in the pastor's chair adjacent to the pulpit with head bowed and hidden, apparently in prayer, was a hooded figure in a simple cassock. Minutes passed. The church chimes rang out at the top of the hour. Thomas turned and looked to see if anyone else had arrived. None had. He was the congregation. *Where is everyone else?* He thought. Then, with a start, he remembered. *Oh, but of course, it is only ten. I forgot to turn back my clocks. I'm an hour early.*

As Thomas eased back in the pew, a trickle of blood ran down the side of his temple and onto the right leg of his corduroys. He wiped the side of his face with the back of his hand. *A bit of a bump,* he thought as he reached for the handkerchief in his jacket.

"Alyosha, you see here, I am just setting the stage. Now, you need to know more about Thomas and his identical twin, Michael."

"Do continue."

The twins grew up in Dixville Crossing during the Depression. After graduating from the local K-12 high school, they both were accepted at Harvard. The athletic director there had caught wind of Michael's athletic heroics in the North Country, as that area of the Adirondack Park was known. Nicknamed OT for Obey Two—a moniker referring to Princeton's legendary Hobey Baker, a member of the hall of fame in football and ice hockey just after the turn of the twentieth century, Michael drew recruiters throughout New England.

As a child, Michael loved action games and developed extraordinary hand-eye coordination. Thomas shared his brother's interest but was not driven to perfection. Michael would repeat drills over and over—juggling, throwing, or hitting balls until he was satisfied with the results. At age sixteen he was developing a slap shot, a lethal way of shooting the puck at the goal, which causes it to rise off the ice at great speed. And Michael loved to run. Any distance. Sprints or up and down neighboring mountain trails. Name the activity: Michael had to be the best among those around him. If he wasn't, he'd work at it until he was. In his teens, Michael heard about Hobey Baker and decided he wanted to model himself after the blond Adonis. So Michael focused on Hobey's two sports, and during his junior and senior years at Dixville Crossing Central School, college coaches came to see him. They left impressed. Ultimately, Harvard offered Michael both a scholarship program and an athletic venue that swayed him to attend there. Michael accepted, providing his twin would be too, for Thomas's talents were only slightly less spectacular. Harvard acceded.

But if Michael had the athletic advantage over Thomas, it was more the result of deference on the part of Thomas, not ability. In both high school football and hockey, Thomas, when the opportunity arose, would showcase Michael. He would throw the block to spring Michael loose for the winning touchdown, run or draw tacklers on an option run, then lateral to Michael for a long gainer, if not a TD. Or in hockey, Thomas would feed Michael the timely pass or put a check on the one player between Michael and the goal. This deference did not go unnoticed by Michael. Each supporting move was acknowledged with a hug or a pat on the helmet. Their respective personas, it seemed, were comfortable with this arrangement.

Yet in the classroom, the roles were reversed. Every year, both were at the top of their class. But it was Thomas who topped Michael. Each was a prolific reader and gifted in math, but Michael always came up just short of Thomas. Thomas simply scored better on exams. Michael might thrive amid physical turmoil because all his actions and reactions were instantaneous and instinctive, but under pressure in a quiet classroom, Thomas held the upper hand.

These were halcyon days for the twins, especially their last two years at Central School. The community turned out for football and hockey games to watch the twins. Football games drew a local following with frequent chants of "OT! OT!" or "Obey Two! Obey Two!" But hockey games played in Lake Placid at the Olympic skating venue drew numbers in the thousands for each game, the chants reverberating rink-side. The twins appeared on radio and in local papers. The football and hockey teams won the North Country Division their last two years, and the hockey team went undefeated. Michael just couldn't be stopped in either sport. He was a scoring machine. He was fast. He was solidly built, so he was hard to tackle in football; he was all but impossible to be knocked off the puck in hockey, and, like Hobey Baker, Michael could carry the puck on his stick at full speed, darting in and out between opposing players, rarely ever having to look down to see where the puck was.

Girls were drawn toward OT as he was the recognized star performer. The twins were strikingly good-looking, modest, and polite. Their hair was jet black, and their bodies well proportioned. They were distinguished by a birthmark that Michael carried in his right eye, giving him a smoldering look the girls found sexy and were drawn to. The teenage girls were more aggressive, embarrassing the twins who remained shy and unreceptive to their advances.

The brothers had never known their father, JC, who had taken off for good when the twins were three, leaving the family to manage as best it could. Their mother, Liz, taught kindergarten at Central School, and JC worked for the state as a road crew supervisor. Rumor had it that one night, a girl in her twenties drifted into town, ending up at Elmo's Bar & Grill when JC was there. They both had a few too many, and the two closed the bar, with JC ushering her back to the rear of the building to what Elmo called his ER room. Featuring a sofa bed where the occasional patron could retire until fit to make it home, JC unfolded the bed and they had some steamy sex before falling asleep in each other's arms. The next morning, JC awoke with this naked full-bodied girl fondling him. He was starving for what she had to give and, being a smooth talker and with his beat-up Ford pickup outside with a full tank of gas, he said, "Baby, what do you say you and I turn our 'hots' for each other into a real adventure? I'll stop at the bank on the way out of town and we'll head, hell, I don't know, anywhere!" And with those words, the girl mounted him, tongued his ear, and whispered, "Honey, you are a real lady killer, aren't you?" Then seeing he was aroused again, she added, "Take me, I'm all yours." What more could a loose girl want who knew how to make her man happy and was accustomed to small-town bars and one-night stands. Of course, JC never let on he was married and had two kids, not that it would have made any difference to her. Some said JC had just had his fill of Dixville Crossing, working on roads and scraping out a living. He was always talking about California, so maybe they headed west. Anyway, that's how his road crew imagined it happened.

Only when the twins were in their senior year did their mother tell them why she thought their father had left. Liz had kept putting them off the few times they had brought the subject up, saying, "Someday when you're older, I'll tell you."

Then one evening after dinner, Michael asked the question once again: "Mom, about Dad . . ."

Liz quickly cut him off. "OK, I'll tell you once and that's it, not that there is much to say and what there is, I'd rather not talk about. He took to drinking more than usual after you both were born. I am not sure why, really. He never said. Maybe it was because we had twins. You two were a handful those first few years. Anyway, it was downhill from there. He stayed out more and more at Elmo's after work. Liquor never agreed with him, even when he just had a few beers with a chaser. But he began to get into it heavily and would come home half-crazed. He made our life miserable. There was a lot of shouting, cursing, and if it was a bad night, he'd beat me and threaten the two of you. This went on for three years. Then one night he just didn't come home. And that was it.

"At the time, I was teaching at school and was secretary at the church. But I still felt abandoned by your father and isolated from our little community. That all changed when Pastor Doolittle retired to be replaced by young John Parks. Up to then, I had rarely attended church services, but there was so much talk about Pastor Parks, the life he had injected into the community, what a wonderful person he was, and how fortunate we were to have had him come to us, that one Sunday, when I was feeling particularly down, I decided to go to the morning service with the two of you. You were ten then and, of course, had no interest.

"I'll never forget that raw November morning. The valley was nothing but shades of gray, snow showers swirling. The church was nearly full when we arrived, minutes before the hour, and there was shuffling as some folks in a rear pew squeezed together to make room for the three of us. Pastor Parks, who was standing by the front doors with the choir, noticed our arrival and came over to welcome us. I'll never forget his manner, the soft reassuring measure of his voice and his eyes, eyes that radiated such warmth. After the service, he greeted the congregation in front of the church entrance, and as he gently but firmly shook my hand, asked if the three of us would join him and his wife with several other families for afternoon tea at the rectory. I accepted. And with that unexpected encounter and invitation, my life was altered, and I hoped yours would be, too.

"In short order, he had all of us singing in the choir, reading lessons, and attending family Bible classes. I thought the two of you would resist, but John, as I was soon calling him, had become involved with school activities—attending plays, debates, sporting events, even sitting in on classes occasionally. Look how he's influenced the two of you. I'm so proud of you both."

Michael and Thomas exchanged glances. "That's true, he's been a positive influence, Mom, but not quite in the way you think," Michael said.

Thomas then added, "He's been great to us, and we like him a lot, but it seems the more we read the Bible, the more questions we have, and the answers we get from Pastor Parks when we turn to him just aren't satisfying."

"What questions? You haven't said anything to me about talking to John."

"We thought it would upset you, Mom," Thomas said.

"Well, I'm curious now, so tell me some of these questions."

Thomas looked at Michael, who shrugged his shoulders. "The cat's out of the bag now, so let's give her some examples of what we mean."

"All right," Michael said. "For instance, Mom, the book of Genesis says Adam lived 930 years, and of the generations that followed, some lived and had children when they were 800 years old or more. In fact, that's all chapter 5 of Genesis talks about."

Thomas then added, "The Bible even begins with chapter 1 of Genesis saying that God made the heavens and the earth in six days. How can these things be true, Mom?"

"So what did John say?"

"He said the Bible is the word of God and is not to be questioned," Michael replied.

"Isn't that true?" Liz said.

"You see," Thomas said, looking at Michael, "there's no point discussing any of this further."

"And why not?" Liz continued.

"We simply feel Pastor Parks's answer fails to pass our litmus test. You agree, Thomas?"

"I agree, Mom."

"So what's this litmus test of yours?" Liz said sarcastically.

"Credibility, Mom, that's all. Credibility," Michael said.

"Oh, you're both too young to understand. You see, faith trumps your litmus test," Liz said with authority.

"OK. Whatever you say," Michael replied, and the exchange ended.

On graduation day, the President's Award was given to Michael and Thomas. As they approached the rostrum to receive their awards, the students, parents, and many members of the community stood and gave a rousing mixture of applause, whistles, assorted hoots and yelps of joy. Among the girls, a number of tears flowed with romantic fantasies for Michael or Thomas now dashed. At the rostrum, the school head quieted the gathering and said, "You both have distinguished yourselves academically, athletically, and as leaders at the highest level. And you are the first students from Central School to be accepted at Harvard University. Moreover, this award has never been given to two members of the senior class, but this year the faculty was unanimous in their support of this exception. Godspeed and God bless."

The twins' first year at Harvard was one of adjustment. They quickly discovered they were not the academic and athletic superstars they had been at Dixville Crossing Central School. As roommates, Michael and Thomas worked as a team to maximize their skills, indoors and outdoors. The twins averaged gentlemen's Cs academically their first semester, and both made the freshman football team, Michael as a defensive linebacker and Thomas as a tight end. Neither played with particular distinction but gave it their best. The team won one game during the season, and all the twins had to show for it were bumps and bruised egos. But Thomas found achievement in his course on religions, scoring his best grade, and Michael had similar results in his introductory course in philosophy.

Michael became consumed by two questions as the semester unfolded: "Who am I?" and "What am I doing here?" He constantly badgered Thomas, asking if there were any answers forthcoming from what he was reading or hearing at his lectures. Thomas's usual reply was, "Well, you know what John Parks would say: 'You are a Christian here to serve God.'" Or sometimes Thomas would offer John's abbreviated response. "'Just keep the faith m'boy.'"

Then one evening, when they were studying together, Thomas said. "You have a minute?"

"Sure." Michael nodded looking up from his desk.

"I'm reading this book," and he held it up, "*The Brothers Karamazov*, by the Russian writer Dostoevsky, that I think would interest you—particularly a chapter I've just finished entitled 'The Grand Inquisitor.'"

"I'm listening."

"Michael, if you could speak to Christ, one-on-one, what would you say to Him?"

"Say that again?"

"You heard me."

Michael thought for a moment and then said. "That's a hell of a question."

"A Roman Catholic cardinal of the sixteenth century has this opportunity in *The Brothers Karamazov*. The cardinal is Christ's grand inquisitor."

"What's the book about?"

"A Russian family in the mid-nineteenth century who wrestle with the existence of God and struggle with how they should live their lives depending on their points of view."

"Absolutely, pass the book on to me when you're finished, O.K.?"

"Only if you promise to read 'The Grand Inquisitor' chapter first."

"Why first?"

"Because, you'll never forget this piece of writing and because it speaks to the numerous discussions we've had about Christian faith."

"I'll read the chapter first," Michael echoed Thomas. And with that they both returned to their studies.

The next day, the Japanese attacked Pearl Harbor.

Mid-year examinations were but a month away. While there had been campus conversations concerning the Axis powers' conquests and at what point the United States would get pulled into a war in Europe, the Pacific or both, Pearl Harbor and Roosevelt's speech before Congress that followed put to rest any lingering doubts; the country would be mobilized.

Harvard students carried on, but all knew their lives would change. In the second semester, the grades of the twins improved, and recognition on campus unfolded as a result of their play on the freshman hockey team. Michael centered the first line with Thomas as his right wing. The big game at season's end was an away game against Princeton with the freshman Ivy League title on the line. Word was out that Michael Clarkson was coming to town with his eyes set on displaying his talents at the Hobey Baker Hockey Rink. The arena was packed, with standing room only, for the encounter. Michael didn't disappoint the crowd, scoring a hat trick in the first period, five goals in all, and with Thomas providing three assists. As the game came to a close, a handful of Harvard fans started chanting "OT, OT" when Michael was on the ice, and when the game ended, a number of Princetonians stood and joined in applauding Michael even though Harvard had won the game and the title.

Then suddenly it was June; the academic year was over. Michael and Thomas enlisted, Michael with the army and Thomas, the navy. They had had lengthy discussions about whether they should join the same branch of the armed forces, but in the end, Michael chose the army and, in August, left for Fort Bragg, North Carolina. Four months later, Thomas departed for Norfolk, Virginia, and the navy.

"After seven months in Norfolk, Virginia . . . , but let me have Thomas tell you in his own words."

"After seven months in Norfolk, where a group of us had been part of an advance base unit in the making, orders came through on March 30, 1944, to proceed and report to the First Naval District in Boston for duty on the USS *Augusta*, a heavy cruiser. We were communications officers and were to become part of that ship's company.

"Subsequently, we sailed from Boston and joined a large convoy of forty to fifty ships heading, as it turned out, for a rendezvous with others in the Irish Sea. We then went on to Plymouth, England, which became our home port before, and immediately after, the invasion of Normandy.

"We worked there until the third week in May, when we were notified that the USS *Augusta* was to be the naval headquarters ship for all naval operations and we were to be on the staff of Rear Admiral Alan G. Kirk, commanding officer of the invasion force, the man in charge of coordinating the actual landing.

"At the last minute, the invasion was postponed twenty-four hours because of an unfavorable weather prediction. I happened to be on duty when the message came through ordering us to transmit the postponement to all ships. This had to be done through the Royal Navy transmitters in Plymouth. I was given the message to deliver to the British, and I was sent ashore in a tender with an armed guard. It was a busy time in their communications office, and it was with some difficulty that I persuaded them that this particular message had to go at once. They simply did not like any US junior officer walking in unannounced and giving an order like this! But they took it. Worried, I returned to the USS *Augusta*, and only when back on ship did I learn that the message had indeed been sent out.

"So we waited the twenty-four hours, which seemed interminable. There was no traffic whatsoever in the harbor, a sharp contrast to the frantic loading of men and matériel of a few days earlier.

"When we set sail the following night, we went east along the coast of England, then turned toward France, moving slowly, our speed set by that of the slowest ship in this huge armada. As planned, the invasion proceeded under the cover of complete darkness, no moon, no lights on ship or shore, save a small white light on the stern of the minesweeper directly ahead of us. Even though I had no communications work to do, there being in effect strict radio silence, my duty shifts remained four hours on, four hours off.

"As the night went on, we began to see some firing along the coast of France and several planes going down in flames. Yet all we could hear was the water splashing shipside as the cruiser cut through the waves.

"Daybreak, June 6, 1944, we dropped anchor off the French coast, and the amphibious landing craft went by in columns toward the beaches to unload troops and equipment of every variety. Advancing to within two miles of the shoreline, one could see minesweepers working the Omaha and Utah beaches. I do not recall precisely when we started the bombardment of German shore installations, but once it commenced, the exchange of fire was ferocious. I had a pair of binoculars that, in odd moments, I peered through. Our landing forces were sitting ducks as the German firepower from atop the fortified cement wall overlooking the beaches was relentless. Men were dropping no sooner than they had landed, often in deep water.

"Shelling from the USS *Augusta* was loud, to say the least, and at times, it seemed that our guns both fore and aft didn't even pause to reload.

"The invasion continued unabated until D-day plus ten, when a three-day storm, the worst in forty years, we later learned, hit us. Gale-force winds with very rough water and pounding rain brought the invasion to an absolute halt. Everyone and everything had to ride it out and wait.

"When the storm subsided, rescue work began. Small craft were detailed to pick up floating bodies, sailors, and others who had been swept overboard or lost in one way or another. The artificial harbors that had been constructed by sinking old merchant ships were cleared and reopened for use. There was still some fire from shore, but the USS *Augusta* was never hit directly. Some shrapnel sprayed the decks from time to time, but nothing caused serious damage to the ship or crew. While danger was ever present, I always felt the ship's armor was such that unless we suffered a direct hit either by a sub or from the air, we would see it through. Day after day, column upon column of ships passed by, unloading their cargoes of men and matériel, only to return to England to reload.

"When the beaches were safely secured, with the invasion force pressing inland, a detail was organized to go ashore. I asked to be included. Destroyed German beach fortifications were still smoldering at Omaha Beach, where we landed. The beach was jammed with men and equipment on the move, and German prisoners were grouped behind several wire enclosures, prisoners who seemed very young and bewildered. Bodies lay scattered around, and I couldn't help wondering if they ever would be recovered, identified, and given a proper burial. And I couldn't stop from thinking, *Where is Michael? Did he land on this beach or nearby? Is he still alive? When will I hear word?*

"The USS *Augusta* remained offshore for almost a month before returning to Plymouth, where I was detailed off the ship and sent to Paris as a communications officer, still with Admiral Kirk, now the commander of Naval Forces France, where I remained a year before returning home.

"Initially, my inquiries to the US Army failed to produce any information about Michael's status. The months passed by.

"Then one afternoon, I received a telephone call from Elliot Ray, a classmate of ours from Harvard, who, like Michael, had signed up with the army at the same time, and who had been able to stay with him in his unit. And yes, Elliot confirmed, they had been part of the invasion forces."

"In advance of the invasion," Elliot began, "a provisional regiment of US Army Rangers, called the Ranger Assault Group, was formed, and two elite units of the group, the Second and the Fifth Ranger Battalions, were ordered to a training center in Braunton, England. Michael and I were with the Second Battalion, Force D, under the command of Lieutenant Colonel James Earl Rudder. On D-day, the Second Battalion landed at Pointe du Hoc, four miles west of Omaha. The beach at Pointe du Hoc was narrow, backed by hundred-foot cliffs above which were barbed-wire fences and German machine-gun nests and bunkers. We were one of the first amphibious landing crafts to hit the beach. As soon as we were unloading and struggling to reach firm footing on the beach, the Germans opened fire from above. It was hell, living hell. We were easy targets as the Germans from the edge of the cliffs machine-gunned round after round down on us or lobbed endless numbers of grenades. Unless you made it to the base of the cliffs, you were totally exposed. Rangers lay dead or dying all over the beach. Somehow, Michael and I were two of the fortunate number to make it to the base of the cliffs.

Suddenly, Michael's voice boomed out above the cacophony around us to a dozen or so rangers huddled nearby. 'Men, we have had the training, and we have the equipment to scale these cliffs. I'll lead you up.' There was silence. Some of the men were visibly shaking. After a pause, Michael added, 'We'll all make it. That's a promise.' Again, silence from the group. 'Listen, we'll fire our grappling ropes with their miniature rockets, get our asses up there, and take out the machine-gun nests, grenade launchers and bunkers, and any goddamn Germans we find. Do you hear me?'

"Then what he said next, I'll never forget as long as I live: 'It is why I am on this fucking beach right now. It is who I am and why I'm here.'

"And Michael fired one of the rockets. The grappling rope uncoiled with a hiss as the hook soared skyward. On the first shot, the hook hung up and held in the barbed wire. Michael pulled the rope tight until he was sure it would support his weight, then up he started. I followed behind him and yelled to the others, 'Remember, he's that college football and hockey star from Harvard, Michael Clarkson. He's a winner.'

"'Let's go!' someone yelled back.

"And up the others went, and damned if we didn't make it, every one of us.

"Coming over the top of the cliff, Michael saw there was a machine-gun nest. He pulled the pin on one grenade and then another and lobbed them, one right behind the other, into the nest. Then he cut an opening in the barbed wire and started helping each of our group up, where we quickly carved out a small defensive position.

"The next thing I knew, Michael was lying on his stomach, dying from a bullet through his back. A stray bullet from the beach? Or a marine that mistook Michael for a German at the edge of the cliff? Who the shit knows? Notwithstanding the complete pandemonium at the time, there could be no doubt as to where the fatal bullet had come from. Our only unprotected exposure was from the beach below. Later, I had a medic dig out the bullet to confirm if it was US ammo. It was.

"Thomas, let me tell you, I am sure none of us in our group would have had the courage to climb that cliff without him leading. Many of us, perhaps all of us, would have died on Omaha Beach, like so many others. His heroism not only saved our lives but also established a beachhead on the cliffs that slowly expanded and eventually forced the Germans to retreat inland. And how is he rewarded? Fatally, by a US Army soldier. Go figure."

As Thomas listened to Elliot, tears welled up in his eyes, his chest tightened, and silently he sobbed.

Emotionally, the weeks following the news of Michael's death were the most difficult he'd experienced in his life. Suddenly, he was desperately, frantically lonely. A depression silently descended like a blanket, smothering him.

Thomas started frequenting Parisian bistros in the evening, haunts on the Left Bank where other US military men were seeking distraction, a laugh or two, or company—company that included single women, women who in some instances not only were there to thank the US GI's with their favors but were trolling for a vulnerable unmarried soldier like Thomas, who might be easy prey and could offer a new life in America away from war-torn France.

At first, Thomas, while drifting from one bistro to another, drank alone, his thoughts returning to Michael and their times together at Central School and Harvard, the numerous exchanges both had had with John Parks, and Michael's refrain, "Who am I, and what am I here for?" Thomas simply could not accept that Michael, as Elliot recounted, found the answers to these two questions at the cliffs of Normandy.

When they were deciding which service to enlist in, Michael had shied away from the air force because of Hobey Baker's fatal air crash at the end of World War I. "I can't explain it," Michael told Thomas. "A premonition, perhaps." Maybe that premonition ended up costing him his life; maybe he would be alive today if he'd chosen the air force in the first place as Hobey had. And Thomas was tormented in his role of simply having been no more than an observer to the invasion.

Darwin was right. Life is all about survival. You need more proof? Christ, two world wars in half a century! Hitler, Mao, and Stalin: there's a trio for you. Not only ethnic cleansing within their own countries and putting to death political dissidents numbering in the millions but also absorbing or eliminating the cultures and people of weaker countries. The Germans had Paris all wired up and were ready to blow it to smithereens as US troops were entering the city. And they had lost the war. All species come and go, and the food chain may change over time, but mankind now seems hell-bent on self-destruction and taking the other life forms with him.

The race is on: who can develop even more powerful weapons to lord it over everyone and everything else? For secular and religious leaders, it is all about power and influence—at any cost.

Did Hobey Baker and Michael see all this in their final hours, witnessing their idealism going up in flames? Did they see the futility, the hopelessness, and the senselessness of it all and, with that realization, opt to check out, overwhelmed with despair?

It seemed so clear to Thomas on the one hand, yet so unclear on the other. Where does God figure into this? Two thousand years have passed, and as a member of the animal kingdom, we should be condemned. If God gave man a "superior intellect," why does he continue to act as if he didn't have one? Darwin would simply say that the primitive animal instincts we like to think we shed remain built into our hereditary genes as powerfully as ever.

"Why is the word of God as set forth in the Bible by competing prophets two thousand years ago so obvious to John Parks but not to Michael or to me?"

"Alyosha, do you feel Thomas's torment? What would you say to console him?" Alyosha shook his head gently and closed his eyes. "Speak, Alyosha, speak. Your faith commands you to do so."

Rubbing his brow, Alyosha finally answered. "Only God can console him."

"And Thomas, what can he do to ease his pain?"

"He can pray."

"Pray?"

"Yes, Ivan, pray to God."

Thomas drifted through his days, with such thoughts bottled up, only to have them surface at evening. He could not escape Michael's loss and his own spiritual confusion.

***

Then one night, that all changed. He was sitting in a bistro, with a vacant bar stool beside him, when out of the corner of his eye, he caught sight of a long, bare, slim, and shapely leg sliding up next to him, a leg belonging to Lisette Fleury. As his eyes traveled up her body, his expectations rose. When the picture was complete, Thomas was sufficiently undone so as to feel embarrassed.

"Occupied?" she gently inquired while settling on the bar stool. Their eyes met, locked, and Thomas's life was changed forever.

Much could be, and perhaps should be, written about the torrid relationship that unfolded between the two over the ensuing months, but to do so would take us far afield from our spiritual journey. Suffice it to say, Thomas had a journey with Lisette all right as the year drew to a close, a journey exposing a sexual desire and capacity within him as well as a variety of ways to enjoy these two he never knew existed.

C'était une affaire de guerre, as the French would say. In Thomas, Lisette saw an innocent, tall and handsome, intelligent American who must be rich because, well, because all tall and handsome, intelligent Americans were rich. If she played her hand well, and so far she was doing just that, she had to become pregnant. And if she became pregnant—well, she was Catholic, and so she would have *le bébé*, and no doubt their love would be even stronger and they would marry; and she would move up and out of her modest Parisian lifestyle, where during the day she could be found behind the counter of a *parfumerie française*, and live the American dream.

In Lisette, Thomas saw a twenty-one-year-old beauty who held nothing back from him, spoke acceptable English with an irresistible

French accent, knew how to dress, could make every evening in bed a new adventure, and held no attitude about *les Américains*.

It came as no surprise to Thomas the following May when Lisette informed him, gently, of course, one night after they twice had shared simultaneous orgasms that she was with child. Two weeks later, they were married in Paris at a civil ceremony. Thomas had written his mother about Lisette shortly after he'd met her and called her a week before they were to marry. Liz cried. Life was moving so fast, she said. First, Michael was killed, now Thomas was getting married. But she recovered, wished Thomas well, and looked forward to their coming home. "Oh, forgive me," she stammered. "You are coming home, aren't you?"

"Of course," Thomas reassured her. "Lisette wants to go to America."

Three months later, they arrived in New York City, where they lingered for a few days, taking in the sights. Lisette exuded enthusiasm, relishing the stores and restaurants, especially along Fifth and Madison Avenues. Then they boarded a train out of Grand Central Station for Lake Placid, where Liz met them.

The brilliant autumnal colors beneath the mountain peaks at Dixville Crossing had just burst forth, and Lisette, after spotting a few chalets, said she felt comforted, as the Adirondacks reminded her of her French Jura Mountains on the eastern border with Switzerland.

Lisette quickly became the talk of the town, and she thrived on the attention. In February 1946, Michael Fleury Clarkson, soon to be nicknamed Miff, was born. Thomas returned to college, not at Harvard but at nearby Plattsburgh, tutoring on the side for additional income. Lisette remained in Dixville Crossing with Liz and the baby, Thomas commuting back and forth on weekends.

During their first couple of years in America, Lisette was occupied with the newborn in Dixville Crossing, Thomas with his studies at college in Plattsburgh. The second summer, Michael's memorial service was held, attended by several hundred, and presided over by Pastor Parks, whose words had eyes welling up, if not overflowing, with tears. Thomas was too moved to speak. In the fall, Thomas returned for his junior year, and from time to time, Lisette went up to Plattsburgh to visit, sometimes with Miff, sometimes without, leaving him in the care of Liz. As Liz became more comfortable caring for Miff, and as he became easier to care for, she encouraged Lisette to venture out with greater frequency.

But the results were not what Thomas or Liz anticipated. Lisette realized she missed the Parisian nightlife, and when she saw that Plattsburgh did not provide what she was looking for, she began to pout. To amuse herself in Dixville Crossing when Thomas was at college, sometimes after dinner with Liz at home, Lisette would go upstairs and change into a tight-fitting blouse and short skirt, throw on a long coat to hide her outfit from Liz, and go and tease the boys at Elmo's Bar & Grill. Mind you, she wasn't looking for action but just driving them crazy, as no one had a body like hers for miles around. And she could knock 'em back with the best of them. Of course, they would buy and try to entice a night with her, but none ever succeeded. She just did it to prove to herself she still had that irresistible *je ne sais quoi* with men. Of course, people talked; but she was French *and* sexy, was having some fun, and it was but a game to her. Even the women had to laugh as the men came home with that looking for some lovin' in their eyes. Elmo was laughing all the way to the bank as his place was jumping most nights in anticipation Lisette might pick tonight to come and light them all up. Of course, when Thomas was in town, business sagged. Thomas and Liz knew of these adventures but said nothing.

Then, after a particularly long, hard winter that left Lisette impatient and quick-tempered, a few weeks before he was to graduate in June, summa cum laude, Thomas took Lisette to Montreal to give her a lift. They stayed in a small hotel in *la vieille cité*, and Lisette responded and came alive. The visit was such a success that, over the summer, they returned numerous times. On one visit, they were having dinner, and sitting next to Lisette on the banquette was a woman eating alone. Lisette brought her into the conversation, and by the end of the meal, Danielle offered to show them spots they hadn't discovered. And so a friendship began.

After this encounter, events unfolded quickly. Danielle, a beauty of similar age to Lisette, was a Québecoise, bilingual in French and English, single, and apparently with considerable financial means, a fact that did not go unnoticed by Lisette. In subsequent visits, Danielle invited them to stay in her spacious and well-appointed apartment, and later in the year, when Thomas found full-time work at George Jackson's Rustic Furniture Store on Main Street in Dixville Crossing, a job that was really seven days a week, Lisette began to journey up alone, taking the two-and-a-half-hour train ride to Montreal from nearby Westport.

As the seasons changed and the winter months with their shortened days descended, Lisette came to have second thoughts about her marriage to Thomas. He was not the rich American she thought she had married in Paris. She now knew that not all Americans were rich. Dixville Crossing was not where she wanted to spend the rest of her life. In short, Lisette longed to have the life Danielle enjoyed. When the two were together in Montreal, they were the toast of the town at an ever-increasing number of parties. And the two agreed that they would acknowledge Lisette's marriage, if pressed, but not that she had a child.

By February, Lisette had several men seriously pursuing her. One in particular was a man thirty years her senior, also married but looking for a trophy wife, and Lisette appeared to fill the bill in spades. And most important to Lisette, he was rich, very rich, oil rich. So when David proposed to her in March, presenting her with a huge diamond ring, which had Lisette sucking for air, she never looked back. When she told Thomas she was leaving him, he accepted it silently, the only surprise being that she wished to leave Miff with him. Thomas knew he could not reverse Lisette's decision to divorce, nor did he care to, after seeing the rock on her finger, which she made no effort to conceal. He would have fought bitterly, though, to hold on to Miff. Thankfully, this he did not have to do. After Lisette broke the news, she left Dixville Crossing for the last time, and neither Thomas nor Miff ever laid eyes on her again.

Thomas threw himself into his new job at Jackson's Rustic Furniture Store and, under George's guiding hand, developed into a craftsman making rustic dressers, desks, tables, lamps, and other furnishings. George was demanding but fair, an able and patient teacher. Thomas continued to live at home with Liz, who resigned her teaching post at the school to devote her days to Miff.

Miff was two and a half when Lisette left. Within five years, Thomas was carrying his weight at the store, business was booming, and George was paying him a salary that more than met his modest needs, as well as those of Liz and Miff. Yet Thomas again found himself in a struggle with depression. Michael's loss still weighed heavily on him, and while he had come to terms with his divorce from Lisette, as a young man's first love affair of infatuation, he worried endlessly about how Miff would be affected growing up without his mother.

***

One weekend afternoon in the spring of 1949, when Thomas was at the store covering for George, who was away for the day making a delivery, a chauffeur-driven, yellow-bodied, tan-top Buick Roadmaster stopped, and a tall, thin, strikingly good-looking man who appeared to be in his late thirties walked into the store. Sporting a blue blazer, charcoal gray slacks, and a freshly pressed white shirt with sweeping wide collars overflowing the lapels of his jacket, he immediately gave Thomas a wide smile and, in a heavy accent, asked, "Mind if I look around?"

"By all means," Thomas replied and then added, "Sure is a stunning automobile. Looks great with the white walls too."

"Why, thank you. Just bought it. Had it driven up from New York City last week. You see, I don't drive. It is a present for my wife." And with that, slowly the man looked over the furnishings on display, again and again letting his hands run over the flat tabletops of varying sizes. "Beautiful, beautiful," he said, and returning to Thomas, who was watching from behind the counter, inquired, "What kind of wood is this, and how do you give it such a smooth finish?"

"Well, the top of the large dining table you're standing by there—it seats twelve—is 150-year-old pit-sawn pine planking. The fine smooth surface is created by applying varnish and rubbing it: first with oil and pumice stone followed by a final rubbing of rotten stone and oil."

"And the chairs?"

"They're steam-bent hickory."

"Amazing. And you do that here?"

"In our workshop behind the store."

"Ah, permit me to introduce myself, Gregor Piatigorsky." The name rolled off his lips easily. "But you may call me Mr. P. Americans have difficulty pronouncing, let alone remembering, multisyllabic Russian names like mine." And Piatigorsky chuckled with the deepest chuckle Thomas had ever heard.

After a brief pause, Thomas said, "Are you the cellist living at Windy Cliff in New Russia?"

"The very one," Piatigorsky replied. "You see, I am especially fond of wood and sensitive to how it is used and treated. My cello sleeps until I awaken it when I play. This plain, pine—planking has come alive under your hands." Before Thomas could comment, Piatigorsky continued, "I'll buy it with twelve chairs. Can you deliver to Windy Cliff?"

"Of course, Mr. P.," Thomas quickly said.

"You are familiar with our castle, as we call it?"

"Only from the outside. As teenagers, in winter, a group of us used to sleigh ride down the driveway. You could go fast if the snow had hardened and iced up a bit. The ninety-degree turn near the bottom sent many of us flying, but it was great sport. I'll tell you one thing. There isn't another camp in the Adirondacks like Windy Cliff. And what a view of the valley and the Bouquet River! You can see for miles. We knew no one was living there that time of year, so we'd climb up the steps to the balcony that wraps around the great hall and peer in the windows to look at the moose head over the fireplace."

"That is just where I want to put this table," Piatigorsky exclaimed, rubbing the tabletop with his massive palms, "right beneath the moose head and in front of the fireplace. And I will share a little secret with you. I have given the moose head a new name. He was called Cliff. Would you like to know it?" But before Thomas could answer, Piatigorsky said, "Vlad. And do you know why I chose that name?"

"I have no idea," Thomas said, asking himself why in the world Mr. P. would think he might have a clue.

"After my dear friend, Vladimir Horowitz. You know the name Horowitz?"

"I'm afraid I don't, but if I had to guess, might he be a Russian musician like you?"

Piatigorsky rubbed his brow. "I think my friend would consider himself a musician. He plays the piano." And Piatigorsky smiled broadly. "Let me ask you, seriously now: would you like a moose head named after you?"

Thomas thought for a moment. He'd just sold the most expensive piece of furniture in the store, and he didn't want to offend Mr. P. and maybe lose the sale. The fact of the matter was Thomas thought a moose was nothing more than a big wild cow, and damn if he'd want a moose head named after him!

What Thomas said next convinced him he was a hell of a salesman. "Moose heads are given prominent places of honor on the walls of Adirondack homes, Mr. P. I think your friend would be pleased with your choice." Thomas couldn't wait to tell George what he had just said.

"You are a clever man. And how do I call you?"

"Thomas, Thomas Clarkson."

"A few years ago, Horowitz visited me at Windy Cliff, and when I told him the name I'd given the moose head, he went up to the imposing head, pulled on its whiskers, and said, 'Now all you have to do is to learn to play the piano.' Perhaps you remember seeing the upright Steinway piano when peeking into the great hall. I told Vladimir to play a ballade for his namesake, and to my surprise, he did just that: Chopin's Ballade no. 4 in F minor, op. 52. And when Horowitz had finished, he lifted his glass of sherry, turned to the moose, and said, 'To your health, sir!'" Piatigorsky let go with a rolling laugh.

Thomas didn't know about ballades; his mind had refocused on the '49 Buick Roadmaster idling outside the store's front door. Piatigorsky, reading Thomas's mind, said, "Come and let me show you my new automobile. Then I'll mind the store for a few minutes and let Johnny, my chauffeur, take you for a ride. Would you like that?"

"Very much so," Thomas said as quickly as he could get the words out.

Two weeks later, Thomas was returning from Fisher Hill and Sol Goldberg's Garondah Lodge in neighboring Elizabethtown late in the afternoon, having delivered a truckload of furniture for the multimillionaire whose claim to fame was to have invented the bobby pin. As Thomas drove down the main street of E-town, as the village was frequently called, he spied the yellow Buick Roadmaster parked in front of the Deer's Head Inn. *A beer sure would go down easy,* Thomas thought, and he might even have a chance to say hello to Mr. P.

Sure enough, in the barroom, Mr. P. was having a drink with Johnny at a small table, and upon seeing Thomas, Mr. P. waved him over and asked him to join them. "Johnny is still trying to teach me how to drive. About an hour ago, I damn near drove the Roadmaster off the road on Route 9 along the Bouquet River. Never again, I said. I'll leave the driving to either you or my wife. Take me to the Deer's Head. I need a Scotch."

Thomas sat down, and after he'd had a beer and Mr. P. insisted he have another, Johnny said he would step outside and wait by the car as people were beginning to gather around it.

Small talk continued for a few minutes, and then Thomas asked Mr. P. how he had happened to come upon Windy Cliff.

"That, Thomas, is a long story. I've owned Windy Cliff for a decade. A friend of mine, Ivan Galamian, who taught at the Juilliard School of music, first brought me up here. As you may know, he formed the Meadowmount School of Music down the road in Lewis for especially talented Juilliard students who would attend during the summer to receive further instruction from world-famous musicians, and he asked me to be the first cello instructor. I had just arrived in New York from Paris and was touring in cities across the country. As soon as I saw this valley, I knew I wanted to have a home here. When I was shown Windy Cliff, it had a look I knew my wife would love, as her family has a castle in France."

"You must have left Paris as the Nazis were approaching?"

"That is true. Jacqueline and I with our daughter, Jephta, may have been on one of the last passenger ships to leave Le Havre before the Nazis took control. Understand, I had been on the run with my cello since I left home in Russia when I was twelve. First, it was the Cossacks under the czar that persecuted the Jews. The Russian Revolution followed and brought the Communists into power, who felt no differently about us. Then Hitler's Nazis swept through Europe. I had no citizenship papers, so my prospects of ending up in a concentration camp and dying were almost certain if I were caught. My only companion during these times was my cello. It kept me alive with money I made playing anywhere I could: first in Russia, then Poland, followed by Germany, and finally France."

"But your reputation as a cellist, I am told, is second to none," Thomas said. "How were you able to develop your musical talent under such circumstances?"

"I came from a musical family. My father played violin, as did my brother. I was given a cello when I was seven. After I left home, I did have some instruction during my travels, and at an early age, I was playing first cello in the Bolshoi Orchestra. But from the time I picked up the cello, all I wanted to do was to play it as well as I could. The cello and I became one. I lived through, survived, and saw the most horrific atrocities humans were doing to one another. Music and my cello were and remain my refuge and inspiration."

"And Judaism? Did it give you spiritual strength?"

"Thomas, do you have any idea what I am talking about?" Piatigorsky said, with eyes that had turned cold and distant. "Have you ever witnessed the ravages of war?"

"At the Omaha and Utah beaches during the invasion of Normandy."

"And what do you think wars are about?"

"You mean what are wars fought for?"

"Yes, what is being fought over, Thomas?"

Thomas reached for his beer, but Piatigorsky quickly laid his hand firmly on Thomas's wrist, preventing the beer mug from being raised off the table. "Answer me, Thomas. Answer me." The pause was too long for Piatigorsky's liking, so he added, "Territory. Territory, Thomas. We're no different from other species on this earth. Religion? Hah! Judaism was, and remains, an inescapable stigma for me. Had I been caught in Russia, Poland, Germany, or France, I would not be here in America today. Oh, the pretenses for undertaking war may vary, religion being one of them, but in the end, it is always about territory. Let me put it this way, Thomas. They will persecute me for being a Jew, but when I am playing the cello in front of an audience, they will not persecute me as a musician. I will be applauded as a musician. And if I excel as a musician, I will be honored. This is true with all great artists, although for some the honors do not come until after their lifetime. Just think how much better the world would be if there were just artists, mostly classical musicians, of course." Beaming, Piatigorsky released his grip on Thomas's wrist.

"One final thought, Thomas, and then I must leave. Jacqueline will wonder where I have gone. Sol Goldberg is hosting a charity event at Garondah this summer to raise money for Meadowmount. I have persuaded my two friends and fellow musicians, Vladimir Horowitz and Nathan Milstein, to join me in two piano trios followed by a

Russian string quartet after dinner. It will be an expensive evening, but I would like you to come as my nonpaying guest. You will sit at my table and see us play together. Perhaps a once-in-a-lifetime opportunity for you. We three world-renowned musicians rarely perform together now. Forgive me for placing myself in that category as well. But as you say in this country: you might as well call a spade a spade. Now, finish your beer." And with a pat on Thomas's shoulder, Piatigorsky stood up and, with a parting wave, said, "I've taken care of our enjoyable libations. An invitation to Garondah will be posted to you tomorrow."

Piatigorsky was right. The evening was a memorable one for Thomas even though he had had no exposure to classical music. He sat between two women, both of whom had frequented the store and who owned several pieces, although they had dealt with George in their purchases. They drank white and red wine as it was poured by attentive waiters. Thomas stuck with beer. When dinner was completed and coffee was being served, Sol Goldberg made his way to a small stage and a microphone that had been set up in the spacious dining area and thanked everyone for supporting the Meadowmount School of Music. He then introduced Piatigorsky. The one hundred or so applauding guests rose as one and did not return to their seats for several minutes.

"Thank you. Thank you," Piatigorsky began. "Vladimir, Nathan, and I are delighted to be here this evening to celebrate the successes of Meadowmount and its role in developing young musicians. Tonight, we have selected three pieces to play for you: first, Franz Schubert's Piano Trio in B-flat major, op. 99, followed by Johannes Brahms's Piano Trio in C minor, op. 101, and finally Sergei Prokofiev's Russian String Quartet no. 2, op. 92, in F major. Two students from Meadowmount will join Nathan and me for the quartet." After the applause had receded for the second time, Piatigorsky continued.

"Before we begin the program, let me say a few words about music. I would not be standing here this evening if it were not for my cello and love for music. I have often said, 'Music makes life better.' And until I came to this country, I lived in constant fear for my life. Robert Schumann is said to have expressed it this way: the troubles of our human existence disappear and the world is fresh and bright again. We will do our best to let our music sing in your hearts."

During the performance, Thomas's eyes moved from one musician to another. How smoothly each played his instrument. How absorbed each musician was. Thomas could see the piano keys, and he was mesmerized by how Horowitz's fingers effortlessly danced across them. Each musician was in his own world made whole by the contribution of the others. There were moments when Thomas's eyes came to rest on several of the oil paintings on the wall behind them: a fall landscape of Keene Valley by William Trost Richards, a summer scene of Lake George by John Kensett, and a seascape by Frederic Church. Each had overhead frame lamps, and the paintings appeared to be even more beautiful than on prior visits to Garondah. Beneath the paintings against the wall was a pine-planked table of his, not unlike the one he had sold to Mr. P. It was then that Thomas realized that all artists shared a common thread, even George and himself.

In the final piece, two teenage Meadowmount students, a slim, tall girl on the violin and a shaggy-haired boy on the viola, joined Piatigorsky and Milstein. If they were nervous, neither showed it. Smiles lit their faces when they had finished, and the audience stood again as applause rained down on them.

The musicians mingled with the audience briefly. Thomas waved to Mr. P., who acknowledged him with a broad smile. Then Thomas took his leave, not knowing that he had laid eyes on Piatigorsky for the last time.

Thomas wrote a note of thanks to Mr. P. and to the host and hostess. Thomas talked one final time on the phone with Mr. P. when he called to tell Thomas he and his family were moving to Los Angeles to join violinist Jascha Heifetz and pianist Arthur Rubinstein in what was to become the premier classical trio in the country, and he had put Windy Cliff up for sale.

Thomas's brief encounter with Piatigorsky had an impact that would last Thomas's lifetime. He began to look at his world differently—the streams, the lakes, the mountains, and the ever-changing sky. There was a beauty he had never really appreciated. George and his wife, Mary, had a camp high on the side of a mountain ten minutes from town with a panoramic view of a nearby four-thousand-foot range. They would invite Thomas up after work sometimes, and together they would watch the shadows lengthen and then cover the peaks as the day bid adieu. On several occasions, Thomas lingered, the sky grew dark, stars came into view, and the moon, ascending slowly, appeared over a peak.

But this beauty ate away at Thomas, as it sharply contrasted with not only the horrors of the war and Michael's death but also the pain and suffering others in the village had gone or were going through in their lives as well. And so Thomas began to think about the void in his own spirituality. He wanted to be grounded. He simply could not believe the Bible was the word of God; too many people were involved in writing and selecting what had gone into the Bible, long after Jesus had left the scene. Thomas knew he wanted to try to find a spiritual rationale that made sense to him. His developing talent as a craftsman, once uncovered, played a decisive role in challenging his thought processes in this endeavor—the arranging of pieces of wood in an artistic way to fashion a functional item of beauty—creating order where there had been none. If he was able to accomplish this with his own hands, then what he was reading in the Bible, hearing in Bible classes, discussing with John Parks, and listening to on Sundays from the pulpit ought to add up in an orderly fashion in his own mind as well. So far it simply hadn't. Other folks believed all kinds of things. That was their business. Everybody's different and can believe whatever they want, as long as others are similarly entitled. So Thomas became committed to finding a spiritual orientation that held meaning for him.

"Alyosha, there is more to tell of Thomas's life and that will come, but I can't refrain any longer from describing Thomas's spiritual encounter."

"Do tell me, Ivan."

When Thomas looked back at the pastor's chair, the seated figure had turned toward him, and a face, still shrouded in shadows, was now fixed on him. *Who* is *this person?* Thomas wondered.

Just then and out of the corner of his eye, he caught a glimpse of Molly trotting down the aisle, tail wagging and moving toward the raised platform. Thomas's first instinct was to call her back, but he remained still. *How'd she get in?* he thought.

As Molly stepped up onto the platform, a hand reached out in greeting, and the hood that had fully concealed the head up to now slid back slightly. The face arched forward toward Molly, and in so doing, became partially exposed. At that moment, a chill passed through Thomas. His jaw went slack. He could feel his heart pounding again. For in that split second, He had revealed Himself to Thomas. He was as Thomas imagined He would be. Molly now lay at His feet, eyes closed, at ease as He gently stroked her head.

Thomas's mind was at once racing and a blur; his breathing and swallowing were labored. "Speak to me," Thomas muttered softly. "Please . . ."

The figure resumed His position before Molly's arrival and now was peering out at Thomas with hands folded in His lap, His face again hidden in shadow.

"Forgive me. Yes, of course, You cannot speak until Judgment Day," Thomas said. "The cardinal acknowledged that, when Dostoevsky imprisoned You in Seville."

"Oh, so you are going to entwine two inquisitors, Ivan?"

"Wait, Alyosha, do not be impatient."

Thomas looked over his shoulder to see if he had been joined by anyone, but no one had come into the church, and something told him no one would, even if they hadn't turned their clocks back. Back at the altar, the hooded figure remained seated, a study in commanding silence.

Thomas continued. "And perhaps the author has a hand in Your being here with me. That would not surprise me. Could it be that you two conversed recently, and he convinced You to make another cameo appearance? He would have a point. You would no doubt agree, for things have gotten worse, in fact much worse. But I am humbled by Your being here. Why, I am not even a Catholic, let alone a cardinal, just an old man nearing his end with thoughts on his mind. Indulge me in a bit of whimsy, using Ivan's poem to frame my discourse with You. Yes! That is how it should be. This time I'll be your inquisitor. Ah, I'm no equal to the cardinal. No, no match at all. Look at how busy he had been the day before You appeared in Seville. Why, he had burned nearly a hundred heretics, a splendid auto-da-fé, to the glory of God. Of course, had any been innocent, they would not have burned; their faith would have saved them. Your church at work. None of those heretics, of course, were worth saving in those days, were they? Not even one?" Thomas looked hard at the darkness that hid His face and went on. "Is it true You did not want to take from us our freedom to choose? Your faith demonstrated by Your refusing the three temptations offered You in the wilderness by Satan? With the passing of twenty centuries of uninterrupted chaos, it seems to me we can question those rejections. Accepting of all or, for that matter, *any* of the three—turning stones into bread, casting Yourself down from the pinnacle of the temple to be saved by angels, or accepting all the kingdoms of the earth—would have caused us to worship at Your feet forever. Seeing the pain and suffering we have inflicted on ourselves and on other species since Your earthly encounter with Satan certainly suggests that Your decision was very ill-advised. You proved Your point with Satan but at what price to all Your creatures?

"Now, instead of having us worshipping You peacefully as Lord and Savior in a harmonious community, confusion, cruelty, discontent, sickness, and starvation—the list goes on and on—run rampant on earth, in fact, accelerate as we fornicate in increasing numbers. You prefer we have *that* choice in lieu of an earthly paradise?

"You overestimated our ability to bridge the gap with the freedom You bequeathed to us, didn't You? It certainly appears so. And once You realized Your poor judgment, why did You not right the error? We continue to make a mess of it all. It is laughable, really. Look at most of the leaders who have been on the world stage the last two thousand years and where they have led us! Just consider a few of Your popes in the fifteenth and sixteenth centuries! Ha!

"And yes, even today Your church, which still claims authority to lead until You return, remains entrenched in its past dogma and seamy scandals, while offering indifferent leadership in dealing with major issues of our times. If judged by Your standards, surely a church deserving failing grades.

"Do You observe all of this shameful behavior and do nothing? 'Let My children be children with their vicious and cruel games?' And then, as if there were not enough on our table, You burden us further with assorted deadly diseases, pandemics, and natural disasters.

"But wait, I am getting ahead of myself. Forgive me. I really want to start at the beginning, the beginnings of Christianity."

"See what I wish to expose, Alyosha, as you will see, are how certain forces, early Christian questions of authenticity, competing religions, scientific discoveries, geology, molecular genetics, anthropology, and archeology have all conspired recently to undermine Christianity. But observe how Thomas presents his case."

"You know what first started me thinking over fifty years ago? Several obvious questions: Your only taking six days, six thousand years ago or so, for the Creation; the two differing accounts of Your divinity as set forth in the four gospels of Matthew, Mark, Luke, and John; Joshua stopping the movement of the sun; the childbearing by the generations of Adam, who bore children in excess of one hundred years and, on occasion, even nine hundred years.

"In my youth, our pastor, John Parks, parried these queries by simply saying the Bible is the word of God and that word is not to be challenged.

"But uncovered historic and scientific evidence quite simply tell us otherwise," I said, "by facts and evidence that were not known at the time the Bible was written."

"'Ah, the word of God must be accepted on faith, m'boy,' he responded.

"And if I cannot find or discover this faith? Who is to blame? Does God reveal Himself to some but not to others? Or as you have mentioned on occasion, one must take a leap of faith to find God. What enables some to make this leap and others not? And does the ability to take this leap separate the good people from the bad?

"Then putting his hand on my shoulder, Pastor Parks said, 'Forgive me. I must go. I have another appointment in the rectory. We will discuss this further at another time.' But we never did.

"I wrestled with these conflicts, but with the passing of time, historical and scientific evidence keeps accumulating, further eroding the pastor's responses to the point it became just embarrassing to bring them up to him again. If, according to the Bible, You had created man as Your final act and bequeathed him intelligence, thereby separating him from the other species of Your creation, why would man's pursuit of intellectual endeavors over the ages be discredited and challenged by Your word in the Holy Bible?

"I'm reminded when my son, Miff, daughter-in-law, Josie, and their daughter, Cody, sixteen at the time, and I were watching the movie *Inherit the Wind* together. Afterward we talked about it. Miff admitted he'd never thought whether the Bible was the word of God or not and refused to get caught up in the discrepancies between religion and science that the movie pointed out. 'They just don't matter to me' was his pat answer.

"'How can they not matter, Miff?' Josie interjected. 'Either the word of God is accurate or the Holy Bible is just a book of good intentions but suffers from misstatements and misrepresentations.'

"'But, Granddad,' Cody added, 'who are we to question God anyway?'

"'You mean question God's book, Cody, for we only know God through the Holy Bible.'

"'Fair enough,' Miff acknowledged.

"'And the Bible was not written by God or Jesus but by various prophets and followers,' I continued.

"'You don't know that, Dad.'

"'That's a historical fact, Miff. These writers were ordinary humans just like you and me but with one big difference.'

"'So tell us, Dad, what was the difference?'

"'They didn't begin to know all the things we know about, with the passing of two to three thousand years.'

"'Such as?' Cody asked.

"'The population of the world, except for a tiny fraction, was illiterate and believed many things we would not believe today. Let me give you an example. Cody, what if I told you I was nearly one thousand years old?'

"'I'd say you were nuts, Granddad. I know you are old but not *that* old.'

"'But the Bible says that Abraham lived over nine hundred years. What if I told you that God spoke to me when I was your age, say back in the Middle Ages, way before Columbus discovered America, and said, "Thomas, I am going to let you live until the beginning to the twenty-first century! A thousand years!'

"'And I replied to Him, "Why?" And He said, "Because a girl named Cody, who would be alive then, and a descendant of yours, won't believe it is possible when you tell her it is true, and you can say, 'See, I am living proof.'"'

"'But Granddad, God didn't tell you that, and I wouldn't believe you even if you said you were a thousand years old. You're just being silly.'

"'Well, as Henry Drummond said to Mathew Brady in the movie,' I continued, "'Joshua didn't stop the sun because we know now the sun is stationary. Joshua would have had to stop the earth from rotating on its axis in order for it to appear that he had stopped the sun, and that's not what the Bible says." And if the Bible was wrong there, maybe the whale didn't swallow Jonah, and maybe . . . well, you see where I am going.'

"Miff, Josie, and Cody remained silent.

"Then Cody offered, 'I just felt so bad for Rachel. She got caught up in all of this, and her love for Burt was nearly ruined. And all he wanted to do was teach biology. If you don't want to believe we come from monkeys, what difference does it make, really? This all happened, if it did, millions of years ago, anyway.'

"'But Cody,' I followed up, 'Brady claimed creation began on October 23, 4004 BCE at 9:00 a.m.—at least according to the theologian Bishop Usher.'

"'Oh, Granddad, Brady certainly made a fool of himself on that one!'"

"Alyosha, are you familiar with the film?"

"Ivan, do let Thomas continue his inquisition with Christ."

"So be it."

The figure in the pastor's chair sat patiently waiting as Thomas gathered his thoughts.

"Let me compare the differences," Thomas began, "between the readers of Your holy book at the time it was written and those of today. To most well-educated people, the unfolding of the universe has taken place over some thirteen billion years, give or take a billion, and the diversified species on our planet are the result of what is known as Darwinian evolution. Moreover, it really cannot be convincingly challenged, with the fossils recently uncovered, that apes became bipedal at least five million years ago and started flaking crude tools leading to the hominid species, *Homo sapiens*, spreading throughout the world, a great migration begun 50,000 to 60,000 years ago out of Africa and culminating some 40,000 years later, evidenced by Y chromosome and DNA genealogy. Or put another way, if man began with Adam, he was an African bushman whose life span, more likely than not, was less than 50 years, not 950 years. And it is naive to talk of our world as a good or evil place. It is what it is: a unique habitat for millions of life forms, life that is extraordinarily varied but limited in duration, depending on the species.

"What have You done in two thousand years to improve Your hand, if I may be so bold while the intellect of mankind has leaped forward?

Nothing. And by doing nothing, You have lost ground. Can't you even tell us how to read Your Holy Bible in the twenty-first century? Certainly, it is not to be read now as it was written then?

"Quite simply, Your church is saddled with hand-me-down scriptures, which You, in Your great wisdom, have left us from two thousand years ago. According to Your church dogma, if there is any part of Your Bible not taken literally, Your house of cards collapses, yes? Your church is locked in the past, oblivious to changes in the world until You come again. And if You do not come to right the ship, Your church will further atrophy, lose its following, and fall by the wayside. For it stands in the way now of unifying a global community, acting rather to divide it, inciting nonbelievers to defy and stand against Your church as we are witness to now.

"Today, in the name of Allah, Muslim suicide bombers take innocent lives of infidels around the world. Christian victims, in turn, counter these terrorists in Your name. Are You stoking the fires on both sides?

"Who can look at what is happening now in the Congo, Niger, Rwanda, Sudan, Uganda, and Zimbabwe, to name a few countries on one continent, especially to the innocent children, and say Your benevolent Father is permitting this under His watchful eye?

"But do not get me going on the suffering of children in the world, millions being sold into prostitution, slavery, sweatshops, victims of AIDS, starvation, and natural disasters. No, let's not go there, for there cannot be any defense for their suffering. Apologies, for I have digressed momentarily.

"As to the matter of how You came by Your divinity, Pastor Parks said, 'Mark and John were simply reaffirming Your Immaculate Conception through Your baptism, as the question of Your divine birth had already been addressed in the gospels of Matthew and Luke.'

"But wait," Mark and John make no reference at all to Your birth; their gospels *begin* with Your baptism. Such a presumption cannot be made. At the very least, Mark and John should have made a passing reference to Your conception.

"Further," I added, "why should these four gospels, selected for posterity by the church founders, leave this matter of Your divinity even the least bit ambiguous? Can it be that Your reported virgin birth is ignored by Mark and John because they did not believe in it and felt that Your Father did not decide on Your divine being until Your baptism when, as all four gospels state, the Holy Spirit—in Luke, the Holy Ghost—descended like a dove on You?"

"You see, Alyosha, the Creation as written in Genesis cannot be taken any more literally today than to say the sun circles the earth. That is a fair comparison, wouldn't you agree?" Alyosha remained silent, and so Ivan continued. "There is no need to say anything, dear brother, so let me proceed to the divinity matter. Yes, I am suggesting that the gospels of Mark and John omit Christ's Immaculate Conception, as miraculous an event as ever took place, purposely. Why? One cannot overlook how splintered Christianity was in its formative years. Judaism did not accept Christ as a divine being then or today. Early Christians, who believed Christ to be divine, nonetheless disagreed as to the timing of Christ's divinity: the virgin birth was one explanation; another was that Christ was 'adopted' by His Father only at the time of his baptism by John the Baptist."

"Then why were the gospels of Mark and John included in the New Testament at all, Ivan, as they only serve to confuse the issue?"

"Listen to Thomas, Alyosha."

"After You had gone, we were left to ponder this conundrum. Moreover, those closest to You, including Your disciples and apostles, couldn't even agree on the meaning of Your ministry. To make matters worse, it appears no one wrote anything down about You for nearly a generation after You left us. You wrote nothing. Your disciples wrote nothing. Paul's letters are the first writings we have, thirty years after Your departure, followed by other gospels, acts, or epistles, as they have come to be known, written at the end of the first century and later by those who, in order to impart veracity and authority, attempted to pass their authorship off as having been written by Your disciples or apostles years earlier. Of course, the uncovering of the Nag Hammadi Gnostic gospels and then the Dead Sea scroll discoveries nearly two thousand years later have only served to fuel further confusion and controversy about You.

"In trying to develop a believable biography, Your followers struggled mightily with how to present Your divinity convincingly and powerfully, bearing in mind the stakes at hand."

Thomas noted that blood continued to ooze from his temple, staining his corduroys. His handkerchief was quite soaked now as he wiped the wound, and in so doing, he felt light-headed. Then a wave of nausea swept over him. "Oh, for a glass of ice water. But that can wait. He wouldn't let me faint here. Now. While I am talking to Him."

The figure in the pastor's chair remained seated facing Thomas, revealing nothing.

So Thomas continued.

"Is it a coincidence that the six major religions today—Buddhism, Christianity, Confucianism, Hinduism, Islam, and Judaism—came into being within fifteen hundred years of one another, give or take a few hundred years? Surely You would not have been so foolish as to have set in motion such rivalries, to have this earth be a religious experiment of Yours, tailored to different cultures in different lands? I think not. Humans had been around for millions of years. Yet these dominant religions were born within the blink of an eye in human history, eons after we had been colonizing the remotest regions of the earth. Not one monotheistic religion, but a handful. Why did You wait so long to come to us? Or is this religious awakening simply another aspect of our unfolding cranial evolution? We needed to explain the unknown as well as have an effective unifier of people: monotheism proved to be superior to polytheism.

"First, there were ancient kings and high priests viewed as gods, expected to deliver to their subjects desirable weather, bountiful harvests, flowing rivers, relief from disease, and victories in battle—to name a few. Over time, as such kings and priests failed to deliver on a regular basis, they lost their aura of godliness, to be replaced by multiple heavenly deities. Mystics, prophets, and revelators followed, acting as intermediaries who claimed to receive visions, visits, and instructions directly from these deities, deities eventually to be replaced by a single all-knowing, all-powerful one, causing polytheism around the world to wither on the vine.

"If You were so generous with Your guidance to prophets of Your chosen people, the Hebrews, why is it you are unable to do so now? Could You not raise Your hand or lower Your head to acknowledge me? You need not say a word."

There was no sign of any kind.

"Very well, I'll pursue my points.

"A holy book evolves, the Tanakh, covering more than a thousand years, setting forth the historical events of the Hebrews, a moral code that we now know as the Ten Commandments, and Your active participation in leading them through persecution, capture, and exile.

"Yet after all they had been through, how is it possible that when You did come, Your chosen people failed to recognize You, taking You for simply another, in this case misguided, prophet? Your Hebrews expected a Messiah king to deliver them, bringing the Kingdom of Heaven to earth, not an unrecognizable commoner who mingled with, and ministered to, illiterate peasants and the diseased, challenging Hebrew leaders and scolding them for misconstruing the word of Yahweh.

"How could You appear so disguised to Your chosen people after all the suffering they had endured for what, a thousand years or more? How could You have asked more of them by way of preparation for Your arrival? Where did they err?

"Then for three hundred years, the Hebrews, and splinter groups who became known as Christians, attempt to make sense of Your two-to-three-year ministry."

"This I find incomprehensible, Alyosha. So much so that I will not even ask you to comment, for there is no satisfying explanation. Let me move on to the divinity question. Listen to Thomas explain."

"You are providing me with an unsettling perspective, Ivan."

Thomas leaned forward, speaking softly now.

"To add further to the confusion, with a handful of disenfranchised followers having anointed You as King of the Jews, the Romans perceive You as a potential threat to Rome, and You are ignominiously condemned to death by crucifixion.

"A series of early Christian apostles, followers, and theologian spinmeisters write treatises and preach their interpretation of Your ministry, known collectively as the Jesus Movement, ultimately reaching the conclusion that You with Your Father and the Holy Spirit form what we now call the Trinity, a monotheistic god that is tripartite. This conclusion is not easily reached. Every card is played by competing Christian leaders in attempts to influence the founding fathers of Your church in Rome of this new monotheism, shrewdly using their political and scholarly clout to discredit rival Christian interpretations by declaring them heretical. Added to this struggle, different languages from the Eastern Mediterranean were involved with translators susceptible to errors in judgment, outright mistakes, omissions, and in some cases even with their own agendas where texts were altered to suit their personal beliefs. And so the credibility of these Christian writings became compromised, if not entirely suspect. But the stakes were high. Very high. Losers in this game of roulette more often than not were fed to the lions or burned at the stake.

"And out of this literary brew, Your word survives? Intact? Alas, this leaves me unconvinced," Thomas said, his hands clutching the back of the pew in front of him.

"What baffles me, quite honestly, is how attentive You were to Your Hebrews prior to Your ministry. They were surrounded by empires vying for territorial expansion and dominance, were continually under siege, enduring hundreds of years of unbearable hardship and abuse, and were praying that You, known then as Yahweh, would come to their rescue and cure the injustices of their world.

"Your prophets saw You not as an amoral, selfish god, indifferent to the human condition like other deities, but as a caring and loving god, involved with and committed to His people's well-being.

"Again, follow the sequence here: we begin with Your ministry of two to three years. Your chosen people reject You. You write nothing. Your disciples write nothing. Thirty years pass before You are mentioned in a handful of letters. Hundreds of years pass before a chronology is in place for Christianity, with who knows how many thousands of players involved in determining this chronology.

"At least dozens of gospels that we know of now, many uncovered at Nag Hammadi, were deemed heretical during the first few hundred years after Your death and eventually excluded from Your Holy Bible.

"Why? Because Your founding fathers in Rome wished us to know You only through twenty-seven writings they determined should form for all time the orthodox canon of Christianity: the New Testament. Three hundred years passed after You departed before this canon was officially introduced by the Roman Emperor . . ."

"Constantine the Great!" a voice boomed forth, from the right side of the platform by the lectern.

Thomas rubbed his eyes in disbelief, for what he saw was a man of medium height wearing a beige toga covered by a scarlet robe, his feet in sandals, and atop his head an ornate crown. Molly started growling, but His hand reached out, He laid it on her head, and she stopped.

The new arrival picked up a nearby choir chair and moved toward where He was sitting, placed the chair a few feet away from Him, sat down, and, leaning toward Him, said respectfully, *"Your Grace, forgive me for running late. But it has been a while since I've had to pay attention to time. I would like to have heard all of what has been said, but I have heard enough to have my say, and I thank you, at long last, for giving me the opportunity to do so."*

There was no reaction from the other figure. No greeting. No acknowledgment.

Turning to Thomas, the new arrival said, *"As you started to say, it was at the Council of Nicaea, where the church bishops convened by me and under pressure from me, resolved that You"*—and with that, he turned and pointed his finger at Him—*"were of one substance with Your Father, one divine being."*

"What the hell is going on?" Thomas mumbled.

"Ah, I'll tell you, old man," the crowned figure said, *"His Grace promised one day he would let me correct, as I see it, the recording of Christianity during my reign. When I bump into His Grace from time to time, I remind Him of His promise, but until today, he has always put me off. Mind you, His choice of this venue, and only you as my audience, leaves a great deal to be desired, but I will make do."*

"Before you begin, whatever you are going to say, who are you?"

"Who am I? For God's sake . . . I just introduced myself! Your Grace, I am deeply insulted. I will not forgive You for this humiliation. Old man, I am Constantine the Great!"

"All right, if you are Constantine the Great, shouldn't you show more respect for Him? You are in His presence."

"Let me explain, old man. His Grace claims to be—no, let me rephrase that—is perceived to be, by some, none other than the Son of God, Messiah

if you prefer. But since I don't agree He is who others say He is, or what He might think He is, I call him His Grace, showing proper respect for His ministry long gone by."

"And He puts up with that?" Thomas said, trying to be serious.

"He does, and I'll tell you why. So let me continue, and all will become clear."

"Get on with it then, but please make it brief."

"When things are clear, old man, one can be brief.

"As I was saying, at Nicaea, we resolved that there would be but one divine being, one substance with His Grace and His Father bound together by what was to be called the Holy Ghost. Not two separate divine beings, father and son. That would be polytheistic, and I had committed myself to Christianity and to the conviction that this new religion could only survive if it were clearly monotheistic. There were bishops who disagreed. So I summoned all bishops within the Roman Empire to come to Nicaea, where I, shall we say, convinced the recalcitrant ones to my view. That is, with the exception of a few, I was successful. And to those bishops who left Nicaea unconvinced, I made it clear that unless they changed their minds, they could expect to be killed and their churches destroyed. After my death, the idea of the Father, Son, and Holy Ghost became known as the Trinity, three in one, and the bishop of Rome before the end of the century declared himself to be the first pope, who henceforth would select the Roman emperor! Who would have believed it, the leader of the persecuted Christians selects the emperor?" Then looking at His Grace, he added in a scolding fashion, *"I am the savior of Christianity, not You."*

"Now stop right there," Thomas interjected. "So you changed the minds of a few bishops, had some killed who did not change their minds, and had a few churches destroyed. Tell me why this makes you anything more than a footnote to the unfolding of Christianity?"

"Old man, do you know that Christianity was all but wiped out before I became emperor? Ever heard of Diocletian?"

"The Roman emperor around your time?"

"He preceded me and left no stone unturned in the persecution of Christians and the destruction of their churches and writings—ethnic cleansing is the term you use today. See, Diocletian had no use for another religion within the empire. Sol Invictus was the Roman sun god worshipped by most cults along with a similar lesser cult, Mithraism. Diocletian viewed Christianity as a destabilizing religious force that had to be eliminated. And he damn near did it.

"But then in 312 CE, I won a glorious battle at Milvian Bridge, soundly defeating Maxentius, who had laid claim to the imperial throne in Rome. Now this battle was pivotal because I single-handedly raised Christianity from the ashes. Did you know that, old man? Does the world today know that? If it weren't for me, Christianity wouldn't be around today, and you wouldn't be sitting in this church talking to His Grace.

"Are you still with me?" Constantine said to Thomas. *"His Grace is tongue-tied, as we know, so I have to take advantage."*

"I'm still with you, but please—"

"Yes, I know . . . I can see that you are not well, but I know His Grace will let me finish our conversation. He made a bargain.

"You see, at Diocletian's death, the Roman Empire was divided. Maxentius laid claim to the imperial throne in Rome and the eastern half of the empire, and I controlled the western half.

"The evening before our military encounter at Milvian Bridge with the imperial throne at stake, I believed my soldiers needed additional motivation. We had had a number of campaigns, traveled far to reach Rome, and my men were dispirited. As the pink sky faded and twilight descended, I was fortunate enough to see the symbol of the Christian cross in the sky. Quickly, I sent out word: 'The Christian God has revealed Himself to me in the evening sky. Paint on your shields His divine symbol, the cross, and He will protect you and lead us to victory!'

"The following morning, not only was Maxentius routed, but my men praised the Christian God for their victory. The word spread among our ranks. Sol Invictus had never come to our rescue in battle, nor had other gods. Then a brilliant idea occurred to me. I had tolerated Christians in the western half of the empire I controlled, and when I pressed Licinius, who succeeded Maxentius, to do the same and we issued the Edict of Milan, Christians obtained the same rights as those of other faiths. Soon after, I defeated Licinius, and the whole empire came under my reign politically, territorially, and religiously. 'This Christian God could be the answer,' I thought. *'A gamble, yes, but worth a try.'*

"My first step was to officially recognize Christians, thereby permitting their numbers to expand. To placate the followers of the official state religion, Sol Invictus, in 321 CE I decreed the day of rest to be 'Sun' day and that Christians who had recognized the Jewish Sabbath on Saturday, shift their day of rest to Sunday. I followed this compromise with another one. His Grace's birth had been celebrated on January 6. The festival of Natalis Invictus, or birth of the sun, was celebrated on December 25 at the winter solstice. Again, Christians fell into line, not wanting to incur any setbacks to the official recognition I had given to them, by accepting December 25 as His Grace's birth date as well.

"This is all true, is it not, Your Grace?" Constantine said with a haughty air. *"Old man, I cannot tell you how I delight in this opportunity His Grace has given me.*

"As one requires a superior strategy in battle to prevail, I believed I must do the same religiously if I were to truly unite the disparate groups within the Roman Empire. People were converting to Christianity in increasing numbers, but I had to have a master plan to avoid religious strife. And the plan I conceived, in my humble opinion, deserves a little more than historical recognition. How about a gospel and one or two psalms for good measure?

"Ah, better yet an epistle. Yes, the epistle of Constantine the Great to the Romans! The Holy Bible would then reflect the role of the two giants, who centuries apart breathed life into Christianity: Paul the Apostle in the first century CE and me in the fourth.

"To refresh your memory, old man, when His Grace died upon the cross, Jews viewed the outcome as confirmation that this figure was not the long-awaited Messiah but simply one of a line of apocalyptic prophets, similar to the second Isaiah who claimed the Kingdom of Heaven was at hand and with it the Day of Judgment. Of course, the predictions of these prophets were meant only for Israelites.

"Paul literally resurrected Judaism, transforming the religion into Christianity. His defining moment as an apostle occurs, as no doubt you are aware, with his conversion on the road to Damascus, where Christ, seen now as the Son of God by Paul, speaks to him, and Paul decides that He died for the sins of mankind. Paul then carries his message to all peoples, not just Israelites, stressing brotherly love to one and all. With this message, Paul travels through Greece and neighboring regions of Asia Minor, with stops in the Mediterranean, ending in Italy. But his missionary zeal might have been in vain had he not maintained contact through his epistles with cities he had visited, epistles serving to solidify his teachings in accepting all who had faith in Christ. The number of Christians grew within the Roman Empire even as persecutions continued. I, of course, not only ended the persecutions but also officially recognized the religion.

"Do I begrudge Paul's seven epistles out of the twenty-seven books in the Holy Bible constituting the canon of the New Testament? Hell no! Paul deserves this recognition. But goddamn it! Ah, forgive me, My Grace. Do not take such language personally." And then in a condescending voice, Constantine added, *"As emperor of the Roman Empire and as Constantine the Great who so supported Christianity that by the end of the fourth century, it had become the official religion of the empire, I certainly should be granted equal footing with Paul.*

"If truth be told, old man, I have written a letter to the Romans, but His Grace refuses to read it. Alas, for centuries it has lain on His desk and no doubt will remain there until the end of time."

Thomas shook his head. "I'll not put up with this charade."

"Charade? A little respect, please!" Then turning to the hooded figure, he said, *"Who am I talking to, Your Grace? Look at him. He's confused, poor fellow. I might as well be talking to this dog at Your feet. I am losing patience. So, old man, let me leave you with other actions taken under my reign.*

"At the Council of Nicaea, to which you were making reference when I arrived here today, we also officially accepted what are now known as the twenty-seven books forming the orthodox canon of Christianity, or the New Testament. Further, the council established the date for the Resurrection and authored the Nicene Creed, which, to this day, is widely used in Christian liturgy.

"I also installed the bishop of Rome in the Lateran Palace, solidifying the structure of the church within the empire.

"Then, as a final act of my commitment to Christianity, I was baptized, in keeping with His Grace, but on my deathbed.

"Now, I have given you the highlights of my reign to dwell on, just the highlights. Ah, but there is one more thing I must address. Earlier, you asked me why I should be considered anything more than a Christian footnote. To the reasons I've just given you, let me add the following. His Grace would just as soon leave things the way they are: the gospels extol Him, cathedrals with their beautiful stained-glass windows glorify Him, the liturgical rites of worship deify him—oh, I could go on and on. The point is, who in their right mind would wish to share this with anyone? And although He won't admit it, His Grace is very insecure. But there is another reason He wishes to keep me under the radar—to turn a phrase current today, and I must say I am quite partial to the phrase—and that is when all is said and done, the survival of Christianity really is due in no small measure to me. This, as I am sure you can understand, is a very touchy subject with His Grace, but that does not prevent me from needling Him about it from time to time. I imagine His reply to me might be, 'But how could I have a man even of your grand stature who murdered his son and his wife be elevated to, say, sainthood?' 'Oh, please Your Grace,' I would respond, 'let us not forget You commanded Abraham to murder his son. And how many Hebrews and Christians have done your bidding with blood on their hands? And tell me, Your Grace, without Paul and me, would You even have the recognition today that Your contemporary, Apollonius of Tyana, has?'"

"Talking to yourself won't get you the answer," Thomas said smiling.

"Until He says otherwise, I'll just accept that His silence is the closest He can come to acknowledging my indispensable role in His survival.

"Now, I must go. I'll leave you in the care of His Grace. He'll decide your fate."

Constantine turned toward the hooded figure, whose eyes were transfixed on him, and, with an almost imperceptible bow, said to

Him, *"I have spoken my piece. The old man is Yours to listen to." And with that, Constantine vanished.*

***

"So you see, Alyosha, in the span of one generation, look at the extent to which the roots of Christianity took hold, thanks to Constantine. The strength and depth of these roots are reflected by the fact that, for the next one thousand years, Europe languished under the iron hand of the Roman Catholic Church, a church consumed with accumulating authority and material wealth at the expense of the populace. This outright greed and corruption during the Middle Ages are unrivaled in denying individual expression challenging Catholic authority."

"Forgive me, Ivan, but I must interrupt again and have you tell me who this Apollonius of Tyana is?"

"Ah, Alyosha, you are listening closely. The name means nothing to you?"

"Apollonius of Tyana? I have never heard of him."

"Nor had I until a philosophy professor delivered a lecture on him when I was studying in Paris, absorbing the new Enlightenment movement. I was astonished by what he said to all in attendance."

"Astonished, you say? Do explain."

"What if I told you," Ivan began, "Apollonius of Tyana was one of the most visible and influential figures of the first century CE, whose life and teachings not only spanned the entire one-hundred-year period but to an extraordinary degree mirrored the brief life and two-to-three-year teachings of Christ."

"Can this be so?"

"For instance, they both purportedly were born in the same mysterious way within a year of each other, caught the attention of their elders at a young age with their religious focus, talked in parables, led solitary and virtuous lives, performed miracles most often by healing the sick and infirm and restoring life occasionally with the laying on of hands, had disciples and followers, suffered persecution, and both were believed to be divine and worshipped as a god by many."

"Ivan, this cannot be true. I would know of this."

"Also pointed out in the lecture, Alyosha, was that Christ is not mentioned until well into the first century CE, through Paul in his epistles. Though Apollonius traveled throughout the Roman Empire, there is no record that he had ever heard of Christ. Oh, then there is the curious connection of Apollonius and the Essenes, the monastic communal Jewish sect with whom Apollonius spent sufficient time to become known as the Nazarene. You see, the Essenes were also known as the Nazarenes, and being early Christians, would they have not been aware of Christ and His teachings? Again, there is no record that they had."

Bewildered, Alyosha slowly shook his head.

"Now let me point out a few of the differences between Apollonius and Christ, which are noteworthy."

"Is there a reason for you to do so?"

"Yes. It can do no harm to test your faith now, can it, dear brother?" Alyosha closed his eyes and sighed as Ivan continued. "Apollonius was born to wealth, then walked away from it. Christ as we know was a simple carpenter from Galilee. Apollonius was exposed to and excelled at his academic

studies, focusing on the philosophy of Pythagoras. Christ's teachings were derived from the modest surroundings he lived in, learning from his life as it unfolded. Apollonius's travels were extensive, crisscrossing the Roman Empire and beyond into the Himalayas, where he studied under Brahman sages. Christ's travels were confined to the area of Galilee. Unlike Christ, Apollonius was a vegetarian, would not drink wine, and would have no part in animal sacrifices. Apollonius was known by and gave counsel to one and all including emperors. Christ's teachings were mostly to the illiterate, poor, and downtrodden, again, in and around Galilee.

"Alyosha, I provide this brief profile to make the following point. Doesn't it seem highly unlikely that two 'divine' figures, overlapping one another within relatively close proximity to each other within the Roman Empire, not only were possibly each unaware that other existed, but it is the lesser-known one who becomes accepted as the Son of God and the other one who is all but forgotten?

"The professor focused his lecture on how hard it is for us to appreciate the impact of the number of not only religions but sects within religions that existed in the Roman Empire and outside her borders at the time of Apollonius and Christ. How could a religion or a sect increase its followers? Through mysterious births, miracles, raising people from the dead, resurrections, eternal life, or—heaven forbid—eternal damnation. These events were common occurrences in those times.

"'Imagine for a moment,' the professor concluded, 'I am presiding over a meeting with fellow founding fathers of the Roman Catholic Church in Rome several months before the convening of the Council of Nicaea. Upon calling the meeting to order, I say to my illustrious friends:

> *Permit me to give an opening statement.*
>
> *As you all know, questions have persisted over the centuries as to how Apollonius of Tyana should be viewed by the church.*

There are those who still steadfastly maintain that he, not Christ, should be recognized not simply as a friend of God but as the adopted Son of God. Once and for all, with your blessing and for the record, I would like to put this matter to rest.

Christ was a Palestinian Jew. The Jews were awaiting the Messiah. They believed Christ was but another prophet and not the Messiah some said he was. Christians believed he was the Messiah, the Son of God, who died for our sins. Apollonius of Tyana was a Greek Pythagorean philosopher. The Greeks were not awaiting a messiah, so why would the Son of God reveal Himself to them?

We do acknowledge that Apollonius's life had much in common with that of Christ, as he too was a virtuous figure, teacher, and healer. And we agree that Apollonius was a holy man. But could he have been the Son of God? We think not. None say he died for the sins of mankind.

But wait, some say we know that there were other crucifixions at the time and place where Christ was crucified. The evidence that the Son of God was one of those crucified is not credible to some. Neither are word-of-mouth recollections by a handful of people thirty or forty years after his death with time to refine, even embellish, such recollections. Is this how God reveals Himself to mankind? Apollonius, on the other hand, was a historically accepted figure, whose life held no mystery—and mystery a deity must have.

What also cannot be denied and is decisive in this matter is that Constantine is inspired by Christ at Milvian Bridge, and in his great wisdom, our emperor subsequently determines that Christianity is a monotheistic religion capable of uniting the

> *peoples of the empire. His blending of Christianity and Sol Invictus, we agree, is a stroke of genius. And as Constantine said to us some months ago, the beauty in Christianity is the mystery that surrounds it! For without mystery, there can be no god.'*

"And with those words, Alyosha, the lecture ended."

"Ivan, your modern version certainly casts an exceedingly long and dark shadow over the Catholic Church during this period, and your introduction of Constantine into the mix raises compelling questions."

Ivan laughed. "Galileo really let the genie out of the bottle in the seventeenth century with his astronomical observations, confirming those of Copernicus that stated the earth was not the center of God's universe as the church had maintained. Since then, the authority of the Catholic Church has witnessed steady erosion. No doubt Galileo would see Christian orthodoxy today as a round of cheese with mice gnawing away at it."

"The mice being . . . ?"

"The modern secular world and all that it encompasses. As I said in 1879, Alyosha, man now seeks to worship what is established beyond dispute. Satan had a better understanding of human nature than Christ. Man wants to be told what to believe, not to have the freedom to choose between the bread of the world and Christ's faith-based spiritual bread. Moreover, Christ wanted this freedom of choice to be made without demonstrations of miracles or acts of divine power. No, Christ wanted man to choose on the basis of faith alone. The cardinal presses the point with Christ when they're in the dungeon: that such restraint on His part was His great mistake, and His church has had to bridge this failing of Christ's by creating an aura of miracles, mystery, and absolute authority. You see, Alyosha, worship in the modern world continues to stretch mankind's sensibilities as his knowledge accumulates. It comes down to a matter of authorship. God keeps giving up

ground. From the earth being the center of the universe, God has been pushed back thirteen billion years to being the creator of what is now called the big bang, with everything since a random and chaotic cosmic expansion."

Thomas saw His left hand rise and His fingers brush His brow beneath the hood, as if relieved Constantine had left. "Constantine certainly didn't mince any words," Thomas said, his voice trailing off, his handkerchief now soaked, his right pant leg stained at the thigh where blood had fallen.

Beads of perspiration trickled down his face. Thomas undid the top two buttons of his shirt. As his left hand returned to his lap, Thomas noticed that he seemed to be losing his ability to focus. The hooded figure was becoming misty; numbness seemed to be setting in on his right side. *Maybe this is it,* he thought. *I wonder, would He let me die right here in His presence?*

"Here, Alyosha, I must return to Thomas's life, and what remains to be told of it."

"Dear brother, you are weaving a tight net."

Miff grew up overnight, it seemed to Thomas. He graduated from Dixville Crossing Central School with average grades and enthusiasm for outdoor sports, like his father and uncle before him. Then he went on to college at Plattsburgh, where he signed up with an air force program at the nearby air base, quickly discovering something he excelled at, and soon, every waking moment he wanted to be in the air.

US troops had been committed to the Vietnam War for nearly seven years, when Miff, in 1968, a few years out of college and twenty-four, found himself in the South China Sea on an aircraft carrier, making forays over North Vietnam in an F-14A Tomcat. On his sixteenth mission, deep into enemy territory south of Hanoi, he passed through some heavy surface-to-air missile fire. One missile found its target, crippling his jet. He ejected seconds before the aircraft exploded.

As unfortunate pilots had before him, Miff parachuted into the hands of the Vietcong and ended up at the notorious prison in Hanoi, dubbed the Hanoi Hilton, where he was held for five years until the end of the war in 1975, having been badly tortured, mentally and physically, during his captivity.

When Miff returned to the United States, he spent a year in a veterans' rehabilitation hospital outside of Washington, D.C. Thomas had been at Andrews Air Force Base when Miff arrived from the West Coast, having undergone initial treatment and debriefing. One by one, the wounded disembarked from the military transport, some on stretchers, some assisted by more able men.

Thomas failed to spot Miff until he was nearly on top of him. "Good God Almighty," Thomas mumbled under his breath. Miff was supported by two military aides, one on each side of him. Thomas guessed about one hundred and fifty pounds hung on Miff's six-foot frame.

Thomas moved to embrace him, but one of the aides put his hand out. "He's a bit unsteady, sir. I suggest you let us escort him inside."

"It's OK, Dad," Miff said weakly. "Jesus, I never thought I would see this day." Tears flooded his eyes, and he started shaking.

"It's over, son. It's over. You're home now," Thomas said softly.

Miff's rehab went slowly. Oh, the weight gradually came back, that is, most of it. But his mind. His mind had been stressed beyond what it was meant to bear. He experienced endless nightmares, where he would wake up screaming. Days where he withdrew completely, wishing the day to end. He was moody, jumpy, and moments away from tears.

At the end of a year, he was told they could do nothing more for him and he'd fare better at home. So Thomas took Miff, still a broken man, back to Dixville Crossing.

It took nearly a decade before Miff could hold a job. Thomas heard that the Lake Placid airport was looking for someone to run its small office as a flight controller and set up scheduling for charters. Miff was hesitant, but he was told they would love it if he would give it a try, and if it was too much, not to worry. After the first day, Miff knew it was what he needed to help him take the next step. Even if he was only around puddle jumpers, as he called the aircraft there, they were planes and they flew. His second week on the job, one of the instructor pilots took him up; it was early in the morning in late September, colors at their peak, not a cloud in the sky, the wind sock limp outside the terminal. For a half hour, they flew above and between some of the Adirondack High Peaks and, of course, took a pass over Dixville Crossing. Then, on the way back to the airport, the pilot turned to Miff and said, "She's all yours." Miff took the controls of the Cessna 172, circled around the village of Lake Placid a couple of times, and brought the plane down with a perfect three-point landing. "Haven't lost your touch, I see," the pilot said.

"You'll never know how much this flight has meant to me," Miff replied. "I left a lot of demons up there. And landing this baby is sure a lot easier than bringing a Tomcat down on an aircraft carrier in rough seas with a crosswind." Before long, Miff was out of the office, flying single-engine and twin-engine charter flights and, from time to time, giving flying lessons. Soon, the word got out that there was a young and single, good-looking, former air force jet fighter pilot giving flying lessons at the airport, and within hours, this word reached Josie Theocropolis, the twenty-four-year-old daughter of a seasonal resident, a Greek shipping tycoon whose family home on Lake Placid was second to none.

The following summer, when the family arrived in mid-June, Josie, who had always had a hankering to learn how to fly, signed up with Miff. Two months later, Josie soloed, and by Columbus Day weekend, she had her pilot's license. By then, the two had become inseparable, a fact not lost on Josie's father, Teddy, who had three attractive, strong-minded, unmarried daughters in their twenties, all of whom he would have traded in for a son.

Miff was everything Josie was looking for. That he couldn't keep her in the lifestyle she was accustomed to didn't bother her in the least. Teddy, however, didn't look at it that way. Once the engagement was announced, Teddy took Miff aside in his spacious study overlooking Lake Placid and offered to set him up with a position in the New York office of Theocropolis Shipping Ltd. TSL, as it was known, was a big player in the transporting of crude oil out of the Middle East via supertankers, and Teddy had a cutthroat reputation with a hair-trigger temper to match. Miff politely declined, only to have Teddy now strongly urge that he accept his offer. Again, Miff declined, eliciting an outburst from Teddy. "Well, you sure as hell aren't going to marry my daughter and live off her money, you son of a bitch."

Miff didn't rise to the bait. "I have no intention of living off your daughter's money. We'll make out just fine. She'll be stepping into my life, I won't be stepping into hers."

"You bet you won't." And with that, Teddy stormed out of the study and slammed the door.

Minutes later, he found Josie by the indoor heated swimming pool. "Marry that guy and I'll disinherit you," Teddy growled as he strode by.

Josie never even looked up from her book as she lay stretched out on a poolside chair but responded, "And tell me what all your money and stuff has done for you other than make you an overweight, angry bore."

Three months later, they were married, and Teddy, true to his vow, disinherited his daughter. Josie was not left penniless, to be sure; she had a little nest egg of her own that Teddy couldn't touch, and while they might not ever own a private jet, a yacht, or a mansion somewhere, they were not going to starve. Miff insisted on a prenup, fully protecting Josie's assets, and Josie, to no one's surprise except Teddy's, settled down and was quite comfortable living with Miff in a low-key Adirondack lifestyle.

Miff augmented his flying income, when the weather closed in and during the winter when business was slow at the airport, by helping Thomas and George at the Rustic Furniture Store. Over the winter, it meant building up inventory for the summer tourist season and finishing promised commission work. George welcomed Miff as, like his father, he was a quick learner, and George, now sixty-five, was slowly turning more and more of the work over to Thomas, eight years his junior and as able a craftsman now as George. The business had grown over the years, to generating nearly seven figures, and had become the most successful commercial operation in Dixville Crossing. Even Teddy gradually had come around to accepting Miff and the marriage, although financially nothing changed, nor would Miff and Josie have wanted it to. In the spring of 1980, Josie gave birth to a seven-and-a-half-pound daughter. They named her Cody.

***

Cody Clarkson sat on an old three-legged stool dressed in only a white nightshirt that came down to her knees. Her long blond hair, tied in a knot when she was captured, now hung loosely to her shoulders. Across from her was the only other piece of furniture in the room, a rusted cast-iron double bed covered by a stained mattress. Her room, which she had measured pacing heel to toe shortly after being confined, was fifteen feet square. A bare light bulb hung overhead. The floor consisted of hard-packed dirt. The walls were bare; the only air entering the room came from a small opening in one corner, close to the ceiling. She had been alone in the room for three days now. Men with covered faces entered and left on no particular timetable to provide her with food and water and empty a pot she used to relieve herself. The food she could not identify, nor was there very much of it. No one had spoken to her, although the men who entered the room stared at her, mumbling to themselves in Arabic and occasionally laughing. She had no idea what might lie ahead. Seeking ransom or a prisoner exchange were two possibilities that crossed her mind. *Good luck on the ransom idea*, she thought. Dixville Crossing might scrape together a few thousand dollars, but from what she'd read and heard, the Iraqis would be looking for millions.

Cody had been huddled with six children in a room at the back of the school. She had become separated from the American and the friendly Iraqi forces when a firestorm erupted all around them, culminating in a huge explosion Cody was certain would bring the building down on top of them. The plan to take back the village of

Mosul from the insurgents had obviously gone awry. The soldiers told her to wait with the children, not to worry, the school had been secured, and they would be back for her. They never returned. Cody and the children remained in the schoolroom even as the firefight slowly abated, then ceased at nightfall. It was then that she heard the foreign voices. The children responded with cries of happiness, and all were swept up and led out of the school into a battered van and driven away. Where they were driven to, Cody had no idea. She was encouraged that the children were now talking happily to one another as they bounced along dusty roads. Her wristwatch and medical supplies had been taken from her, but they were of little use now. All she knew was that when the van came to a stop, they seemed to be far from Mosul. She and the children were then separated; she was taken into a small building to the room she now occupied.

The first night, Cody dozed. For whatever reason, she did not feel in physical danger. Why would they want to kill her if American dollars could be obtained or an exchange arranged for imprisoned Iraqi combatants? She doubted that an abandoned nurse in a schoolhouse with some preteen-age children would be viewed as an American spy. The insurgents might even want to take advantage of her medical skills to assist with their injured fighters. The following morning, a woman dressed in a burka with only her eyes showing through her veil came into the room and, with hand motions, asked her to put on the clean nightshirt she had brought with her. The woman left when she felt that Cody had understood so she could change in privacy. Shortly, the woman reentered and motioned her to raise her nightshirt to her head. Cody did as directed, revealing that her panties and bra had not been removed. Again, with hand motions, the woman conveyed that these two pieces of apparel were to be removed as well. Cody shook her head vigorously. The woman rubbed her hands together over the pot on the floor in a way that Cody understood she only wanted to wash the items.

Cody again shook her head.

The woman left. Minutes later, she returned with four men whose heads were covered by black silk head socks with narrow eye slits. One of them pointed first to the burka-dressed woman and then to his three companions. The message was clear, do what she says or we'll do it for you.

Cody turned her back to them, dropped her panties followed by her bra. The men left, with the woman carrying the undergarments.

On midmorning of the fourth day, she heard her door being unlocked, and an insurgent officer—at least he appeared to be an officer, dressed in military uniform and without any head covering—entered and addressed her in English.

"Please accept my apologies for these modest accommodations, but we are at war and the Americans have destroyed many of our villages and homes. I will sit here," and the officer pulled the stool away from the wall. "You will sit on the side of the bed," and he motioned her to do so. Cody obliged. "I could have come the evening I brought you here from Mosul or the following day, but you see, the question was what were we to do with you? I have been thinking about that, and last night, the answer came to me, providing you met—how should I say it—certain criteria."

"And what are the criteria you are looking for?" Cody asked with a voice that failed to hide her apprehension.

"You had to be blond, pleasing to the eye, young, and . . ."

"And what?" Cody said, as the officer paused.

"A virgin," he said matter-of-factly.

What Cody said next even surprised her. "So you want to turn me into a whore?"

"No, that is not what I have in mind, at least from my point of view. I'll ask you to listen closely to what I am about to tell you and remain silent when I am finished. I will give you a day or two before requiring an answer."

Oh my God, Cody thought. *Oh my God.*

"You see, Muslims believe that a better world, in fact a heavenly world, awaits them after they die. For the men, particularly those who sacrifice their lives or become martyrs, when they ascend to this heavenly world, each Muslim male knows that he will be immediately welcomed by seventy-two vestal virgins who will care for him and fulfill his every wish. As you are aware, much of our success in defending our country from you American invaders is due to our suicide bombers. Bringing down the World Trade Center towers gloriously demonstrated the impact of this strategy to the Muslim world. You call these men terrorists. To us, they are heroic figures who will be honored by Allah forever. The Qur'an says so.

"I will not go as far as to say that Allah came to me last night in a vision, but I do believe it was He who spoke to me in a dream I had, where He said, 'I have sent to you the woman you have captive. Muhammad, she is one of My seventy-two virgins to be used as a preview of coming attractions of what awaits My martyrs in heaven.'"

"He's got to be kidding," Cody said under her breath. "He's mad! I'd rather die."

"I will not turn you into a whore, my dear, and I'll tell you why. You will be only giving gratification to young, virgin teenage boys who are about to sacrifice their lives to Allah. You will be worshipped by these children because of the love, affection, and gratification you will give to them. You will be seen as one of Allah's angels who has been sent by Him to remove any doubts they might have as to their giving up their lives within days after they have been with you. These boys will never have experienced the love that you will give to them. I don't like to use the English word *sex*, although that is what we are talking about here. You will awaken them to the sensual pleasures of love. You will overcome any of their inhibitions because you are an angel. They will do what you want them to do, no doubt hesitant at first, some embarrassed, but you will devise ways to bring them to orgasm. I will have a woman in the room with you for those evenings a boy is with you who will act as translator and report to me on your achievements. Perhaps I may even serve in that role to see that you are giving it your all and the boys are so pleased they have to be dragged away from you. I will tell each boy, 'Allah sent me one of His angels to be with you. Now you must please Allah. He will have not only this angel but seventy-one others just like her waiting for you in heaven who will be with you forever.' Let me end by saying that you will not be receiving boys in this room but in one you will find quite luxurious, since an angel must have suitable surroundings.

"And if you refuse to do this, you might be thinking, what happens? The alternative you will not like, my dear, but I must tell you so you can weigh the pros and cons of my request.

"We would start with one of the six schoolchildren who accompanied you in the van and who are all safe in a nearby home. But as you no doubt are aware, girls are expendable in our world. I would bring one of them to this room and, in front of you, subject her to pain such as she has never felt before, for you to witness with your eyes, and with your ears, her screams. We would continue this slow torture until she died, perhaps in a day or two. You would have to live with the guilt of this child's horrific death. If there was no change in your thinking, a second child would be brought in and subjected to a similar ordeal with the corpse of the first child by her side. And so we would continue until you could not bear the screaming and the smell any longer. Do you want to be needlessly responsible for one or more of these miserable deaths? All for refusing to gratify some virgin teenage boys who will see you as an angel? And let me add, it would be foolish for you to think I am bluffing. We excel at this business of slow torture.

"Now, I will leave you to your thoughts. I will visit you tomorrow morning at this time, and if you have not made a decision, I will give you until the following morning. Only on the second morning, I will enter with one of the girls and several hooded men with tools, equipment, and acid. Your answer the second morning must be immediate or else the torture of the child will begin and not stop, regardless of what you say, until she is dead."

Cody turned away from the man and buried her face in the mattress. The following morning and after a sleepless night, she told him she would be the angel he wanted her to be. "You will not regret your decision" was all he said, and left.

That evening, after she had eaten, she was blindfolded and moved to a second-floor bedroom of another building in the village. The room was spacious in comparison to where she had been held. There were two lounge chairs, a couch, a table with four wooden chairs, and a double bed with a canopy out of the *Arabian Nights*. In one corner, a small fan moved the air laden with incense around the room. A nondescript well-traveled Persian rug covered half the floor. When Cody pushed back the curtains over the two window spaces, she was confronted by vertical bars. The room was lit by two bedside standing lamps and one table lamp. After the men had taken off her blindfold and left, she tried the door, which, of course, was locked. She retreated to one of the couches to wait. For what? A virgin teenage boy to enter the room, with a translator, to meet an angel?

She did not have to wait long. But it was the officer who entered the room alone. "Ah, my angel, you like this improved setting? Yes, I think this will work nicely. Too much light for my liking." And he went over to the lamp on the table and turned it off. "Yes, you look even more sensual. The boys will not be so afraid."

"So when is the first boy presented to me?" Cody asked. "And how do I satisfy you in doing what you wish of me?"

"I will be your teacher. I will show you what I expect, for you are a virgin and do not know of the ways of love. You *are* a virgin, yes? I would know by now if you were not." Cody said nothing. "Well, it is not that important, since tonight I will find out whether you are or not."

"No, no, not you," Cody gasped. "You never said I would have to be raped by you!"

"A mere oversight," the officer said softly as he approached the couch. "Please." And Cody moved more to one side so he could join her. "You do not have to worry as I am not married, and I have only raped young virgins in defending Islam. I will be gentle, and you need only do what I tell you. The quicker you learn lovemaking from me, the sooner you will play with the young boys and enjoy yourself while doing it. At least, it must appear so to me or whoever is in the room with you. Will it be awkward at first? Of course. But in time, less time than you think, my dear, you will become immersed in your role as Allah's angel."

"But I won't be a virgin to these boys then. Allah will not be pleased," Cody offered weakly.

"True, but the virgin boys will not know for they have never had sex with a woman before. But time is passing, and I wish to start the first lesson."

"When?"

"Tonight. Right now. I desire Allah's virgin gift to me." Then the officer leaned over and took Cody's full and shapely body into his arms. "Come, come, relax. Do you want to see one of those schoolchildren brought upstairs instead of pleasing me?"

"Oh, God, give me strength," she said to herself as tears came down her cheeks.

"One small request before we begin," Cody pleaded, with his arms holding her close.

"Of course, what is that?"

"Your name? Tell me your name."

"Muhammad Aboud Sayead," he replied.

"And what shall I call you?"

"Muhammad."

"Ivan, please . . ."

"Alyosha, again, hear me out."

Muhammad Aboud Sayead was born in Riyadh, Saudi Arabia. His father, an engineer, had left Iraq to work for the bin Laden family, prime contractors to the royal family of King Saud. As an only child, Muhammad grew up listening to talk of Osama bin Laden, one of the sons of the family patriarch. It was when Osama was asked to leave Saudi Arabia because of his ongoing radical remarks against the royal family and formed the terrorist organization al Qaeda in Sudan, that Muhammad's interest in following in the footsteps of his father as an engineer waned. Al Qaeda's terrorist activities in Sudan soon became so successful and praised in the Arab world, and the organization's existence and Osama's own life put in such danger by threats of retaliation by the United States, that bin Laden fled Sudan and set up al Qaeda bases in Afghanistan. Muhammad then decided he wanted to join Osama and his cause and he knew whom to turn to in Riyadh to join up. Soon he found himself in Afghanistan at one of the al Qaeda bases undergoing training in terrorist schooling. Six months later, he was ordered to the United States to join part of an existing al Qaeda cell in Jersey City, New Jersey, across the Hudson River from downtown New York. Without incident, Muhammad slipped into the United States via Canada and joined four others in a modest apartment to await further instructions.

Although there was one member of the group who served as their instructor and taught them a good deal about explosives and a variety of possible terrorist schemes, they had idle time on their hands. Sufficient funds were wired into an account at a nearby bank every month allowing them to explore and experience the decadent modern world that Islam wanted to destroy. They were not drawn to museums, operas, ballets, classical music, or Broadway shows; rather, their tastes leaned toward local bars, massage parlors, strip joints, and, when confined to the apartment, pornographic movies. They even talked about bringing prostitutes to the apartment, not to bed but to entertain them, but Muhammad was afraid matters might get out of hand with such decadent infidels. While the Qur'an permitted any activity if it were to further the cause of Islam, Muhammad's religion also only approved sleeping with a Muslim virgin at marriage. At eighteen, he had never made love to a woman, although in his time spent in America, he discovered what turned him on. The cell had been in Jersey City a year when, on 9/11, the world changed. In disbelief, the five watched on television the two World Trade Center towers burn and collapse. "Glory be to Allah," they repeated over and over at the scene they were witnessing. Later that day, a call came ordering them to return immediately to Afghanistan via Canada traveling separately, the first leg by car to Montreal. All made it back without incident.

***

On the morning of 9/11, Thomas was in Lake Placid reclining on a dental chair in preparation for a routine cleaning, when the hygienist, entering the operatory room where Thomas was waiting, said she had just heard that a single-engine plane had crashed into the upper floors of the North Tower of the World Trade Center. She offered no other details than how odd the incident was, considering the New York area was enjoying a cool and cloudless fall morning.

The hygienist had finished cleaning Thomas's upper teeth when the dentist, Dr. Bradlow, stopped by the room and announced that the upper floors of the South Tower also had now been hit by a plane. Further he added, the two planes had both been identified as commercial jets, apparently hijacked by al Qaeda terrorists, and it was feared more hijacked jets were in the air with other targets in mind. Dr. Bradlow turned to leave, paused, and then said, "Thomas, Hutchins & Hutchins Real Estate on the floor below has a television. Let's go down and see what in God's name is going on."

Thomas checked his wrist watch: 9:15 a.m.

When Dr. Bradlow and Thomas arrived at Hutchins & Hutchins, the door was open and a number of people were standing in front of the TV. "Dave! Come in! Come in! Look at this! It's unbelievable!" Fred Hutchins said to Bradlow.

Thomas could not believe what he was looking at. The upper floors of both towers were ablaze. From the large hole in each tower where the commercial jets had entered, giant flames spewed out, and from the surrounding windows, now without panes, poured volumes of thick black smoke, all but obscuring the tops of the two towers. Every now and then you could see people jumping from these windows, opting to die from the fall rather than be incinerated.

As the minutes passed in the offices of Hutchins & Hutchins, only barely audible words could be heard: "Oh, my God!" "Look at *that*!" "Jesus," and the like.

Thomas looked at his watch: 9:30 a.m.

Minutes later a third jet hit the Pentagon. "God Almighty," someone said. "What is going to be next?"

A half hour later, there was a scream from someone in the room. "Dear God, the South Tower is collapsing!" In seconds the tower was no more—only swirling clouds of smoke, dust, and debris enveloping the city blocks surrounding the World Trade Center complex. Twenty-five minutes later, the North Tower came down in similar fashion, leaving further blinding, suffocating, billowing clouds. Those people caught under the covering blanket of destruction but fortunate enough, one way or another, to emerge injured and/or in shock were covered head to toe as if they had been engulfed by volcanic ash. Many did not emerge and lay dead or dying on the streets and walkways. Ambulances came and went. Firemen, officials and their vehicles, overwhelmed by the magnitude of the catastrophe, did what they could.

Thomas walked over to one of the windows in the real estate office and gazed upon the mountain known as Whiteface, towering over the surrounding peaks, as cumulus clouds floated across a cobalt blue sky. The contrast between what he was witness to on television and what he was looking at from the window at Hutchins & Hutchins Real Estate defied comprehension.

It was now believed one or two more hijacked jets were still airborne. At the time, there were some four thousand commercial flights in the air over the United States. How do you find the one or two out of four thousand? And if you identify the one or two, how do you bring them down with civilian passengers aboard? This news came out piecemeal. Eventually, it was determined there was but one other hijacked jet, and it had crashed in a Pennsylvania farm field killing all aboard.

Thomas remained by the window looking at the landscape he so loved while anger came to a boil inside him. "What is this world coming to?" he murmured.

"I don't think we want to know," said a woman close by with tears in her eyes.

For the next two years, Muhammad lived as a fugitive, moving from one mountain cave to another along the northern border between Afghanistan and Pakistan, withstanding heavy bombardments from the United States and occasionally involved in ground firefights. Following the invasion of Iraq and the capture and hanging of Saddam Hussein, Muhammad wanted to return to his native country as an al Qaeda member to assist the militant Shiite cleric and political leader Muqtada al-Sadr, whose forces were proving to be a formidable resistance to the American invaders. Muhammad's knowledge about explosives and familiarity with Iraq, he argued to his al Qaeda superiors, could be useful. So with their blessing, and as the American surge was under way in Iraq, Muhammad returned to Baghdad, where he was born.

His uncle, a mullah, welcomed Muhammad warmly, as did family friends. Muhammad told his uncle he had returned to do whatever he could to help defend his country and spoke at length of his al Qaeda training and expertise with the latest and most powerful miniature explosives, especially those triggered by cell phone devices. The religious leader listened intently and told Muhammad he had recently been approached by an al-Sadr aide who was looking for someone with Muhammad's knowledge to create powerful devices suicide bombers could wear or place in vehicles. These suicide attacks had been very effective and disruptive, getting worldwide attention, when successful. The problem had been that too often the devices failed to detonate or the suicide bomber got cold feet when en route to his destination and abandoned the mission. Muhammad said his talents were meant for such assignments. The religious leader said he would contact the al-Sadr aide and tell him of the return of his nephew and their conversation. The wheels were soon put in motion as the al-Sadr aide responded quickly and positively; they definitely could use Muhammad if he would operate out of his apartment in the suburbs, for his Sunni targets would be in Baghdad and Tigrit, Saddam's seat of power. Al-Sadr militia members would deliver the explosives and devices to him for assembly, and, once they were assembled, Muhammad would ask for a vehicle to carry his deadly cocktail to the designated target with the chosen suicide bomber. Most would be teenage boys native to neighboring countries, as families in those countries, opposed to the presence of US forces in the Middle East, received large sums of government money for sacrificing their children, especially their sons; other children's families were devoted believers of the Islamic faith who would offer their child as a suicide bomber for martyrdom, without payments, believing the entire family would become martyrs. Only infrequently did an Iraqi family offer up a son for money when Saddam was alive.

When Muhammad was ready, Mosul had become the hot spot for intensive fighting; the insurgents controlled the town, the marines and Iraqi forces intent on recapturing it. The day Muhammad arrived with an explosive-laden van and a suicide bomber, the focus of the opposing forces was a schoolhouse. Civilians, teachers, and children had taken refuge there, believing it was as safe a haven as any. After a prolonged firefight, the marines, including a medic and a nurse, seized the school. No sooner had the marines deployed their group in the building so as best to withstand a counterattack than there was a massive explosion, blowing away the front half of the school. Most of those inside were killed or severely injured. A group of masked insurgents entered what was left of the unstable structure, rushing from room to room and firing at will. The nurse, who was at the rear of the school with six unattended, stunned, crying young girls, took them to a maintenance shed away from all the turmoil.

As evening fell, the firing all but ceased. Muhammad was then given permission to go to the school and see the impact of his work. When he arrived, he was told it was too dangerous to enter from the front, sections of which appeared on the verge of collapsing. He noted the huge hole adjacent to the school, where the explosion had occurred. Only fragments of the van lay scattered in the area. The suicide bomber would have felt nothing. Then a voice from the schoolhouse shouted for him to walk around to the rear of the building to "get some children and a woman out of here."

***

Holding her close as he leaned over to her, Muhammad's moves were awkward. He kissed her on the neck, but Cody was unresponsive, turning her head away from his. Her mind was racing. *This can't really be happening to me,* she thought.

Muhammad's hand moved up her bare leg as he said, "Trust me. You have been sent to me." Then, after a pause, he added, "I lied. I am a virgin, too."

"And you are going to teach me about sex?"

"One year in your country, I have learned all about the pleasures of love."

"If you are a virgin, how have you learned these pleasures, as you call them?"

"I have learned from your sex movies, magazines, massage parlors, lap dancing clubs. Shall I go on?"

"Oh God."

"TV. Pay-per-view. *Playboy*. Hugh what's-his-name and all his women with huge breasts, where they swim nude in the swimming pool in his mansion and have sex and sleep with one another."

"All right, all right, I've heard enough."

"Very good. Now let me show you what I've learned. Why shouldn't two virgins who believe in God enjoy each other?"

"Who said I believed in God?"

"You wouldn't have carried a small Bible with you if you did not believe in God, now would you?"

Before Cody could respond, Muhammad's cell phone rang. His jacket lay across an arm of the sofa. He reached over and retrieved the phone from a pocket. The conversation was brief. Cody did not understand a word, except that several times Muhammad uttered "OK." When the call ended, he stared at the phone as if considering what to do next.

Then he said, "I must leave. Now. Iraq is at war. I will return when my assignment has been completed."

"How long will that be?" Cody replied in a voice of relief.

"A few days, a week. Maybe never. That is in Allah's hands."

"And me?"

"You will be under the care of my uncle, a mullah. I will speak to him of my new assignment. My cousin, Azadeh, who has been bringing you your meals and lives downstairs, will check on you, too." With that said, Muhammad left.

The following afternoon, the door to her apartment was unlocked, and Azadeh let in a tall, thin, slightly stooped elderly man, who, she guessed, could be none other than Muhammad's uncle. Dressed in a neck-to-ankle robe buttoned at the top, sandals, and an *amameh* atop his head, he had the typical white beard. In one hand, he held her Bible and, on his other arm, a beautiful cockatiel with gray plumage, a distinctive yellow head, and orange-red ear markings. She guessed the parrot was a foot tall. The mullah motioned her to one of the chairs at the dining table and then seated himself at the table across from her.

"Muhammad said to bring you this," he said in a slow but clear English accent. "I am Muhammad's uncle." Then he gently slid the Bible over to her. "He thought you would like something to read in his absence until we decide what to do with you."

"Thank you," Cody said, realizing that Muhammad had not told his uncle what he had planned for her.

"And to entertain you, I have brought my cockatiel, Sheytoune," and he motioned to the bird with the hand that was now free. "Azadeh will bring his cage with fruits and seeds to his liking, if you care to accept this companion. He will amuse you during the day. At night, you cover the cage with this cloth I have with me, and Sheytoune will be quiet until uncovered. He is tame, as you can see. He will enter his cage when taken to it."

Cody was at a loss at this offering. "I don't know what to say" was all she could manage, before adding, "You trust me with Sheytoune? Me? An infidel?"

"An infidel you may be, but a nurse of any faith cares for people and animals, yes? However, if you do not like parrots, I will take Sheytoune back with me."

"No, no, I would love to have Sheytoune to keep me company. You are most kind. And I will care for him as you have instructed."

"Excellent," the mullah replied. "Sheytoune enjoys being read or talked to. When he starts warbling, he is telling you he has heard enough. He is well versed in the Qur'an, as I read to him daily in Arabic from it. Normally, we do not give infidel prisoners anything to read, but in your case, I make an exception because you were protecting six Muslim children when captured and carried with you your holy book. It will comfort you, yes?"

"It will comfort me," Cody replied simply. "And again, I thank you."

"My pleasure," the mullah said and then added, "Your Bible is a good book but not the word of God. The Qur'an is the word of God. God spoke directly to the prophet Muhammad. Then, God's word was written down to become our holy book, the Qur'an. Jesus was a prophet, too, but no one wrote down anything he said until perhaps what, thirty, forty years after he died? That is why God had to speak to Muhammad six hundred years later: to be more precise with His message. It is logical what I say, yes? Otherwise, why would God have spoken to Muhammad, and have the Bible followed by the Qur'an, if He was pleased with His word in the Bible?"

The mullah had given Cody her Bible and Sheytoune, so she had no intention of engaging him in a religious discussion that might cause him to change his mind and take back his two gifts.

"You state your preference for the Qur'an clearly and with conviction," Cody offered gently.

"Ah, that is why I am a mullah," he beamed. And with those words, he rose from the table, placed Sheytoune on her arm, and departed. Cody heard the key turn, once again locking the door.

"Well, Sheytoune," Cody sighed, "You have me now, like it or not."

Sheytoune looked around the apartment carefully and then said, "I've seen worse."

"The bird knows some English!" Cody said in astonishment.

"Some English!" Sheytoune replied mockingly as he walked up her arm to her shoulder. "She insults me. Insults me!" Then, leaning toward her ear, he added, "My dear, I am quite fluent."

Cody turned her head to look at the parrot. His yellow-crowned cocked head and one of his brown eyes were now inches away from her face. *The bird is carrying a hidden microphone,* Cody thought as she lifted Sheytoune off her shoulder and returned him to her arm.

"Let me ask you a question," Sheytoune continued as if reading her thoughts. "Why do you think Allah gave parrots vocal abilities? You humans think you are the be-all and end-all. All parrots can do is mimic a few phrases, right? Wrong. It took Alex, the African gray, to give you all pause for thought. You've heard of Alex, haven't you?"

Cody nodded slowly, still shaken and stunned by what was taking place.

"By the way, what is your name? Now that we are conversing, don't you think I should know your name?"

"It's Cody. Cody Clarkson."

"Cody Clarkson," Sheytoune said several times until he had it just right. "I like that name. Has a nice ring to it. Easier than Mahmoud Ahmadinejad. Too many syllables. Get tongue-tied trying to say his name."

"Well, I'm relieved to hear your speaking skills have not reached perfection yet, Sheytoune."

"Careful. Careful now. I sense envy in those words." And with that Sheytoune started preening his right wing.

Cody attempted to keep the dialogue going, but Sheytoune kept saying "Later, later," while he continued with his preening. Azadeh brought Cody lunch at the usual hour, then returned with Sheytoune's cage. Some nuts and fruit were in his dish, and the parrot immediately responded, "About time, about time." Then he entered his cage, picking out and eating the particular combination of offerings pleasing to him. When Cody and Sheytoune were alone again and both had finished eating, Sheytoune announced from his perch, "Nap time, nap time," his eyes half-masting at first, then slowly appearing to close.

Later in the afternoon, Sheytoune's curiosity about Cody returned. "Nap's over, so where do you hail from, Cody? 'Hail from,' I bet you didn't think I had that in my linguistic repertoire." And with that he let out a loud squawk.

"'Linguistic repertoire.' Give me a break. Nothing surprises me about you now, Sheytoune. I hail from America."

"So you are an infidel nurse from America. Wow! That makes you quite a catch. And the mullah brought you a Bible. Not good. Not good at all. Where in America?"

"Dixville Crossing."

"Where's that?"

"In the Adirondacks."

"Oh, I know where they are," Sheytoune said proudly.

"And just how do you know that?" Cody said, rolling her eyes.

"A wide variety of birds are year-round or summer residents in the Adirondacks."

"That is true, Sheytoune. I am familiar with many of them. My favorite is the pileated woodpecker. There is a pair who live in the woods next to our house. Often we hear them with their distinctive call or see them in flight giving the impression they haven't quite mastered the technique. Our family has always had feeders throughout the year."

"It pleases me to hear so."

"And you, Sheytoune, where do you hail from?"

"Australia."

"Oh, my! So how did you end up with a mullah in Iraq?"

"I'll tell you, if you will tell me how you did, too."

"A deal."

Sheytoune scratched his left ear and then said, "I was doing what all parrots in the wild do in Australia, when one day a group of us got caught under nets thrown by exotic bird hunters. With the casting of those nets, my life changed. Ugly. I don't even like to think about it. First, our wings were clipped so we could never fly again. Then we were put in cages so small you couldn't open your wings, or what was left of them. Our cages were filthy. Food and water were hard to come by and never enough. Half of us died from starvation, lack of water, heat, or stress. Those who survived were soon separated and then sold. All this happened when I was ten years old. Six years have passed, and during that time, I have been bought and sold many times. Twice, I nearly died. I've been in all kinds of cages, all too small. New owners initially treated me well, or as well as they could. But soon they would lose interest, forget to feed me or give me fresh water or clean my cage. The worst part has been having no cockatiel mate to be with. We're groupies by nature, not loners. When I see birds fly by outside a window, imagine how I feel. I've lived in Malaysia, Indonesia, Vietnam, India, Saudi Arabia, and now Iraq. I was a gift to the mullah. I think he accepted me because I was being kept by a member of Hussein's Republican Guard, and during the invasion by your country, bombs were exploding day and night. The mullah said I would be better off with him living in the suburbs of Baghdad."

"Baghdad! So I am in Baghdad!"

"Yep," said the parrot. "Now tell me about you."

"Not all that much to tell, really. Was born and raised in this little village in the mountains. When I graduated from high school, I went on to a college that had nursing courses. Then 9/11 happened. You know about 9/11, Sheytoune?"

"Yep," the parrot again replied.

"Well, a few years later I volunteered to serve in the military over here. You see, my granddad served in the navy in World War II and my dad in Vietnam. Runs in the blood, I guess. I was embedded with some marines in Mosul when I got separated from them while protecting six Iraqi children, was captured, and here I am."

"Now we're both caged, aren't we?" Sheytoune said.

"Scary, when I think I may never see my family again."

"I gave up ever seeing Australia a long time ago. Live off the memories. As for being scared, that fades away in time. Boredom follows. That's worse."

"But we have each other now. I'm not scared anymore, and you aren't bored, right?"

"Yep, so let's enjoy each other while it lasts." And with that, the parrot returned to preening, which meant he was finished with conversation. Shortly after dinner, Sheytoune perched on his roost in his cage and repeated "Bedtime" several times, so Cody covered the cage with the cloth and soon both of them were asleep.

The following morning, the mullah stuck his head in the door to see how the two prisoners were doing, said "Good morning" to Cody, and then left. Suddenly, a series of explosions occurred, close enough to shake the house.

"Damn war! Damn war!" Sheytoune squawked. "What's the point? Senseless killing. And if you're not killing, you're destroying everything." Then a particularly loud explosion nearby set their ears to ringing.

"That was close," Cody interrupted.

But Sheytoune's line of thought was not to be broken. "People are overrunning the world, Cody. It's that simple. We see it looking down through the fouled air. Migratory routes are disrupted, food chains disappear, forests vanish, the land is scarred, our numbers diminish and even vanish."

"I see it in the Adirondacks, too, Sheytoune. Birds, animals, and trees are suffering. Acid particles fall when it rains or snows, contaminating the water and food supply. It's awful. Pollution is everywhere. But what's to stop this madness?"

"Let's see how many ways we can think of."

Cody paused, then said, "A pandemic wiping out half the people on earth."

"That's a good one. Let me see . . . What about a volcanic eruption for the ages that would blacken the sky with soot for years?"

"Or being hit by an asteroid," Cody countered. "That would really do the trick."

"Or a nuclear war with all the countries owning a bomb getting in the act."

"Now, it's getting tough." Then Cody added, "This is a little far-out, but what if there was a total financial meltdown, civil unrest, and worldwide anarchy?"

"Got me on that one," Sheytoune said, scratching his neck. "High finance is not my strong suit."

Before the conversation could continue, a series of bombs went off as US jet fighter planes roared by overhead, this time rattling items in the room where the two prisoners were held. These raids went on all day and into the night, making sleep hard to come by.

The next morning, the mullah came again and took Sheytoune with him. All he said was "He will be safer with me."

During the ensuing month, Cody's life took a turn she never could have imagined.

Muhammad returned. He had been badly beaten, and the commanding presence he had had when he left was gone. Cody treated him with medical supplies from her knapsack Azadeh held downstairs. At first, Muhammad did not want to talk about what had happened, but as she nursed him back to health, the barriers between them slowly softened. In a way Cody was yet to understand, Muhammad had become isolated in the world he was living in and apparently was as vulnerable as she was. Without acknowledging it to each other and as each day passed, they drew closer to one another. Then one afternoon, Muhammad told her al Qaeda had held him captive and beaten him because his training of suicide boys too often had led to failure. They still either fled in the vans loaded with explosives and blew themselves up on some bumpy road in the middle of nowhere, killing no one but themselves, or they triggered the detonating device prematurely en route to their target, killing only a couple of people, not the eighty with fifty more severely injured as planned. Al Qaeda had counted on him. He would reverse his results, or he would die. He had one more chance.

Al Qaeda gave him three targets to be hit in sixty days; they could all take place on the last day, but the hits must be successful. He'd be given one month to recover from his beating, then a month to assemble explosives and train three boys provided from underground sources. Muhammad's confession to Cody removed the final barrier that had been keeping their relationship at arm's length.

He had confided not only in an infidel but in a woman. They saw each other now as man and woman, not Muslim and Christian, and as they realized what they had in common, their differences slowly melted. In a period of days, there was more sustained eye contact and innocent yet encouraging touching. Then one afternoon, when Cody was serving tea to Muhammad, the cup slipped from her hand, spilling into his lap; he leapt out of his chair, letting go a yelp. The next thing they knew, they were in each other's arms. "Oh, I'm sorry, so sorry," Cody mumbled.

Muhammad held her head. Then he kissed her. Cody threw her arms around him, and before the day was over, they had morphed into young lovers exploring and enjoying each other with unchecked passion.

The days flew by. They couldn't see enough of each other. But al Qaeda had given Muhammad a deadline, and he had to address Cody again on the predicament he was in, not with al Qaeda, but with her. As it turned out, it was Cody who brought the subject up. Her solution: they should work as a team with the objective of his escaping from his association with al Qaeda and her being freed and turned over to the US military. If this could be done in concert, so much the better, if not, then in a way so they could be reunited after the two objectives were achieved. What she also said, stunning Muhammad, was that she would be willing to be the vestal virgin for him now, feeling the results justified the means. Now, Muhammad had second thoughts about his vestal virgin dream sent by Allah; Muhammad didn't want teenage boys enjoying sexual pleasures with Cody. But in a bizarre twist, Cody, her sexual desires confined until released by Muhammad, was excited by the idea of gratifying teenage boys whose desires had been similarly confined. "You cannot go against Allah's wishes. If Allah wants to save you through me for the efforts of your suicide bombers, then God does, too, since God and Allah are one and the same!" Muhammad had no answer. Then Cody added, "I will give them so much pleasure that they will run to you when I am done, knowing that in a few hours all seventy-two of us will be waiting to give them anything they want for eternity."

So Allah's dream was implemented. Cody, with Azadeh's help, turned the one-room apartment into an Arabian room of sensual pleasures: lots of reds, incense, soft lighting, and Arabic music. Then, when the day came, Cody made herself up into what she imagined a vestal virgin might look like.

At this point, Alyosha, who had been quiet for some time, interrupted with unbridled curiosity, "Ivan, you have piqued even my interest. Tell more about this vestal virgin you have in mind."

"I know, you want me to tell you what she looks like in the buff, a phrase appropriate for my modern fable, yes?" Ivan paused, then said, "Let me

answer you this way, Alyosha. I remember seeing in Paris, at the time I wrote my original version, a woman who aroused all my senses, whom I couldn't take my eyes off of, and when she spoke, I hung on every word, whose every movement captivated my attention, and when she looked at me, spoke to me, and smiled at me, completely undressed me, made me light-headed, and without even thinking about it, I would have gone to the ends of the earth to please. Then, after sharing a bottle of fine wine, I thought of what she would look like in bed after we had slowly undressed each other, and as her perfume enveloped me, I would look at her and say, 'You are the most beautiful, sensuous woman I have ever seen.'"

"So tell me what she looks like, Ivan. I want to be able to picture this vestal virgin."

"Ah, that is for you to picture, dear Alyosha, for such beauty is in the eye of the beholder."

The young boys came to Cody, usually one a week, sometimes two, if a second vehicle could be made available and explosives assembled. The boys would come to the apartment late in the afternoon, having bathed and been given a robe by Muhammad at his apartment nearby. Although each boy's virginity was almost a certainty, Muhammad pressed each one, assuring them that if they were not virgins and were lying to him, the vestal virgin would know and tell Allah, and seventy-two vestal virgins would not be awaiting him in heaven. Instead, he would be taken away by Satan to join the infidels in hell.

The day before the first teenage boy was to arrive, Cody suddenly realized there was a problem. How was she to communicate with him? In a panic she voiced her concern to Muhammad. "Will you or some stranger be in the room with us to translate what is said in Arabic as you initially assured me?"

"Do not worry," he replied. "I have taken care of that. Allah will speak to him when he is with you and will guide him if needed. Divine intervention."

"Please, Muhammad, be serious!"

"I am quite serious. Allah sent the dream to me. Now, he will assist in executing it to perfection. No more questions. Once the boy enters the room, you are never to say a word to him the whole time he is with you."

"No way!" Cody said in disbelief.

"No, just my way," he replied. "You'll see."

The following evening, when Muhammad arrived at the door to the apartment where the vestal virgin awaited, sixteen-year-old Khalid was shaking. Muhammad told him that he could not go into the apartment with him because Allah would permit only Khalid to view the vestal virgin, and once he entered, he should go to the chair on his right, sit down, and say nothing to the vestal virgin until Allah spoke to him and told him what to do. With that, Muhammad unlocked the door, and Khalid entered the room, furtively looking at Cody before sitting on the chair as directed. Cody had been in high school plays a number of times, and teachers always commented on how she threw herself into the roles she took. *Well,* Cody thought, *I have no idea how a vestal virgin would perform, but then no one else does either, so anything goes, I guess.*

As she smiled at the boy, a deep Arabic voice filled the room. "Khalid, Allah is speaking to you. Say 'Praise be to Allah.'"

Khalid repeated the words so softly they could hardly be heard.

"Louder, Khalid, Allah did not hear you."

"Praise be to Allah," the boy said more forcefully.

"Very good. Now I want you to listen to me very closely and do what I say. The vestal virgin before you will not speak to you. Vestal virgins do not speak on earth. I will speak to you and tell you what to do, and you will do what I say, do you understand?"

Khalid nodded.

"I did not hear you, Khalid," the voice that filled the room said.

"Yes," the boy replied.

"Excellent."

As all of this was taking place between and Allah and Khalid, at first Cody was hard-pressed to keep a straight face. Then, with Allah still speaking, the boy got up from his chair and approached her where she had been reclining on the bed in her best Cleopatra pose. *What in God's name did Allah have in mind?* Cody asked herself. Was she just supposed to lie there and passionately welcome Khalid into her arms?

To Cody's amazement, Khalid responded to Allah's instructions at first nervously but soon with smiles and enthusiasm. She fulfilled her role satisfactorily if not with passionate abandon. At one point, when Khalid showed that his sexuality had been unleashed, Allah praised her in English.

Succeeding rendezvous with what Cody was now referring to as her "boy toys" became more spontaneous as she recognized each boy's particular reservations in being intimate with a vestal virgin, although one boy toy fainted when he saw the vestal virgin and, when revived by Cody, fainted a second time when Allah spoke to him. But Allah was unfailing in his supportive but essential role. Allah had certainly become familiar with the decadent ways of the modern world. Cody didn't know where the microphone was hidden, nor did she care. What she couldn't figure out was how Allah could observe what was going on when he was not in the room. She got nowhere on that one, as Allah would only say that "at all times, He sees everything."

Muhammad met his deadline with a week to spare. Six of nine suicide bombers hit their targets as instructed. Al Qaeda was so impressed with Muhammad's results that they said he must continue a while longer, as the United States had initiated what they called a surge and al Qaeda was losing control of the Ramada territory, which had been their stronghold, and they were under pressure elsewhere as well.

Over the next three months, the preview of heavenly coming attractions of Muhammad and Cody continued unabated. Then she became pregnant. For six months, she kept it a secret, not knowing what Muhammad's reaction would be. But during that period, al Qaeda continued to lose its influence over the Iraqi people, not only in Ramada but across the country; suicide bombing no longer was an effective strategy. Muhammad was told to cease his operations and return to Afghanistan, as things were heating up there. He had had enough. He wanted to return to Saudi Arabia and take Cody with him, a wish fraught with danger for both. Not only would there be danger during the journey, but also in attempting to get across the border. It would be far easier and more convenient for Cody to turn herself over to the US embassy in Baghdad. But then what would she say she had been doing all this time, and how would she explain her pregnancy? She certainly could not take Muhammad, an al Qaeda operative, with her to seek asylum.

When the day finally came and she told Muhammad she was with child, he was furious. Why had she not told him when she first knew? Whose child was she pregnant with? Muhammad panicked. Suddenly, everything they had shared evaporated. Cody was now not only an infidel woman but a pregnant American whose child would be his as well, whether he was the father or not. He had to get the hell out of Baghdad as soon as possible, head south, and cross the border into Saudi Arabia and home, where his family would welcome him back a hero.

Muhammad left the next morning. There were no parting words to Cody. He told Azadeh that al Qaeda needed him in Afghanistan. That was where he was going. Allah would take care of him. She should look after the American woman until their uncle decided what to do with her.

Nearing the Kuwaiti and Saudi borders, Muhammad ran into a British checkpoint a few miles north of Basra. He was asked to provide identification. A problem: the vehicle he was driving was not in his name but that of Taja Hatoum. What followed were a series of questions that Muhammad handled nervously. The British took him into custody at their garrison outside the city. There he was subjected to more interrogation when the British ran Hatoum's name through their database. Unfortunately for Muhammad, the database revealed that Hatoum was an al Qaeda operative. The British, in turn, handed Muhammad over to the marines, who transferred him to Abu Ghraib prison. When sufficient information was not forthcoming, they sent him to an undisclosed country, where there were no restraints on how information was obtained. Within days, when Muhammad as mastermind for many suicide bombings had been extracted, through the use of torture outside the Geneva Convention, he was again transferred, this time to Guantánamo, Cuba, where several hundred alleged terrorists were being held. No one knows the treatment he received while confined there. For sixteen months, Muhammad languished at the prison, and with no resolution in sight, he took his life by cutting his wrists one night with a small but sharp piece of metal he had found in the barbed-wire outdoor pen. He died slowly but peacefully in a pool of his own blood, knowing he had served Allah well and would be rewarded in heaven.

The mullah came to Cody the day Muhammad fled. Azadeh had gone to him before the dust of Muhammad's departing van had settled. She told him all she knew and begged forgiveness that she had not confided in him sooner. Sobbing uncontrollably, Azadeh said she had been sworn to secrecy by Muhammad, who had told her Allah had given him a vestal virgin to further the Islamic crusade against the infidel Americans.

When the mullah saw how the apartment had been transformed since his earlier visits, he needed to know no more. He had a quick look, said nothing to Cody, and left. The mullah's mind was made up before he returned to his house. The next day, men with stockings over their heads came to the apartment, had Cody put on a burka with veil, and bound her hands. The same was done to Azadeh. Hastily, they were taken to a nearby dusty field where two pits had been dug. Two piles of small stones had been assembled about five yards from the pits. The women were placed in the pits until the mullah arrived a half hour later. With him was a crowd whose faces were also concealed. In Arabic, he said, "These two women have defamed Islam. Praise be to Allah." And with that, he picked up two stones and threw one at Cody and one at Azadeh. None in the crowd knew who was being stoned or why, other than that, according to the mullah, the two sentenced had defamed Islam.

Death by stoning does not come quickly. The mullah departed as soon as he had thrown his two stones. Cries for help yielded to groans, whimpers, then silence. When the piles of stones had disappeared, the stone throwers left. No one checked to see if the women were alive or dead. No one returned until the next day, when the bodies were buried in the pits. Two days later, the mullah fled, never to be heard from again.

Miff and Josie had spoken to Cody the day before she offered to be embedded with the marines; she called them once a week. When two weeks passed with no word, they became concerned. Cody had given them the name and cell number of Richard Eller, the son of Dixville Crossing summer residents, Bill and Dana. If communications broke down with Cody and they became worried, Richard had offered to be the contact for Miff and Josie since he too was in Iraq, as a freelance journalist. In fact, Richard had become a celebrity in town due to his frequent appearances on the NBC evening news. He'd even met with President Bush in the Oval Office, providing firsthand updates of the Iraq conflict.

Miff put a call through to him. "I've been trying to see if anyone knows what happened to Cody," Richard told Miff. "It seems the marines got caught up in a firefight in Mosul with the insurgents. Cody was with them. The marines had just secured a school in the center of town when the front of the school was torn apart by explosives in a vehicle driven into the school's entrance by a suicide bomber. That's all I can tell you. As soon as I hear anything more, I'll call you."

A month passed, then two. Miff and Josie refused to believe the worst. When Cody was growing up, they marveled at how she loved to hike, climb the High Peaks (as forty-six of the mountains were called), fish the lakes and streams, or camp out, especially with her grandfather, Thomas, and then, when she was older, more often with other classmates or on her own. Even in winter, she would climb the snow-laden peaks, snowshoe or cross-country ski in the valleys, and, yes, camp out on occasion, too. When she was ten, a doe was struck and killed by a car near the town, leaving a fawn at her side. Cody nursed, fed, and raised the deer. Two baby skunks were abandoned, and she took them under her wing until they could fend for themselves. Her love and care for wildlife was what led her into nursing. After 9/11, she knew where she should be—with the US armed forces in the Middle East.

Miff's years in Vietnam came rushing back. Once again, he was in front of a firing squad, being fired at with blanks. Twice he had gone through that ordeal. He never knew if some of the guns were loaded. It was a game. Some pilots were killed. Others cracked and suffered nervous breakdowns. You never knew if tomorrow was going to be the day they carted you off to an unmarked grave. Miff dreaded what Cody might be going through, if she was still alive and in the hands of the insurgents. Richard e-mailed every two weeks for several months. His last e-mail said simply, "The marines have listed Cody as missing in action." With this news, Miff's tortuous memories when in his cell in Vietnam consumed him, and Josie couldn't stop crying.

Miff and Josie would never know what happened to Cody.

When Thomas heard Richard's news, he, too, retreated into himself. For weeks, he was only seen in the early mornings, having coffee and toast alone at the town diner. His mind was churning. He'd lost his brother in a world war; his son had suffered greatly and never was the same when he returned from Vietnam. Now his granddaughter had most likely given her young life in Iraq. Over three generations, nothing had changed other than that there were more people in the world to fight over what they wanted.

To Thomas, politics and religion seemed inevitably to translate into power, greed, corruption, and, ultimately, conflict. And with each new generation, weapons become more deadly. Who is fooling whom? This has been going on since man became bipedal. Ha! Do what needs to be done to prevail.

George had retired on his seventy-fifth birthday, turning his store with two assistants over to Thomas and Miff. Liz never remarried, and Thomas continued to share a small cottage with her a few minutes outside Dixville Crossing, until Dana entered Thomas's life.

After Lisette, Thomas had never been keen on anyone else, passing on several opportunities that might have led to relationships, but in truth, prospects in Dixville Crossing were limited. To the group at Elmo's, Thomas had done all right. They would not forget Lisette Clarkson, but he was more comfortable now at home with a book in his lap than at Elmo's with a drink in his hand.

Dana Eller changed all that.

William and Dana Eller had been a fixture in Dixville Crossing for many years, appearing Memorial Day through Columbus Day. Bill's family had been coming to the hamlet for three generations. The Ellers were thought of fondly within the community because of their involvement in and financial support of the school and

Dana's participation in several village arts groups; she was an art teacher at a high school in Baltimore. They had one son, Richard, who made occasional appearances in Dixville Crossing between assignments.

The Ellers had a modest summer residence on the side of Pilgrim Mountain, with a sweeping western view of the valley and, when nature was so inclined, offering breathtaking sunset panoramas that Dana would often put on canvas. Invariably, a number of these and other Adirondack scenes of hers would be on sale at the furniture store. Beautifully set off in frames made by Thomas, the paintings were bought up as soon as they appeared in the store.

Over the years, Bill and Dana had purchased pieces of George's rustic furniture for their residence, or camp as they called it, and no doubt some of these were by Thomas's hands. Curiously, Thomas had never met Dana. She had always dealt with George up front in the showrooms, while Thomas and the other assistants were hard at work in an adjacent workshop.

Two events brought Dana and Thomas eventually together. A year before George retired, Bill had a heart attack while hiking and died before he could receive proper medical attention. Everyone was stunned, as Bill, just sixty-two, had no history of heart problems and appeared in excellent health. By then, Thomas handled customers in the showrooms on a full-time basis. One day, Dana poked her head in the door to see if Thomas would continue to display her paintings under the same arrangement she had had with George. Thomas, of course, welcomed this overture.

Initially, the professional interests that brought George and Mary and Thomas and Dana together expanded to their spending evenings socially, then taking side trips. Dana, a widow now for five years, being in her mid-sixties, had all but decided that she would not wed again. She led a full life with her artistic interests, community involvements, and a wide-ranging group of friends.

Secrets in a hamlet like Dixville Crossing are short-lived; Dana and Thomas were soon the talk at the diner over breakfasts and at Elmo's come evening. But the couple couldn't have cared less. Their personalities complemented each other perfectly—Thomas, strong, quiet, and laid-back—Dana, vivacious and hyperactive. They shared mutual interests in their outdoor activities, cooking, and fireside evenings indoors or curled up with a book when not socially engaged. In short, Dana was a delightful companion, but being a seasonal resident, the winter months moved more slowly for Thomas. He recognized their relationship had local parameters and depended on the participation, affection, and support given by George and Mary. Summers were to look forward to.

Occasionally, when they were alone on summer evenings, the two would discuss their respective feelings on life. They talked about religion. Dana considered herself a pantheist, a faith she summed up as, "When you see a beautiful sunset, you feel something you don't feel when you drive into a shopping mall." Thomas laughed when he heard that. "As for church," she added at another time, "the only reasons to attend, as far as I'm concerned, are to enjoy the beautiful music, choir, the architecture, if noteworthy, and to let your soul, your inner bear—as I like to refer to it—be massaged by the colorful rituals. Alas, the church in Dixville Crossing is short on the latter two. Ministerial translators, I do not need. And I would like someone to explain to me why taking communion is necessary more than once a year? If you take it daily or every week, as some do, what is the incentive to improve yourself during your lifetime if you are forgiven of your sins the next day or a week later?" Sometimes, Dana's approach could be offensively blunt: "No one has *the* answer," she'd say. "Born-Agains drive me crazy. The arrogance in saying their way is the only way, and if you don't get it, *you* have a problem, and you'll fry in hell when you're done here. Give me a break; Jesus was inclusive, not exclusive, for Christ's sake. But at least in this country, they haven't reached the point where they use their children as suicide bombers, rape women, and cut off heads of nonbelievers for worldwide television viewing."

Thomas's view on the subject was more reasoned: "We know what took place historically and what scientific discovery has uncovered. In each case, as we keep finding out more about our past and more about the world around us, knowledge continues to accumulate with increasing speed, undermining the dogma of faith-based religions. This dogma has failed to reconcile convincingly the widening disparity between knowledge and the leap of faith religions ask—a disparity that was far easier to bridge two thousand years ago."

The eight years Thomas spent with Dana passed, it seemed, in a matter of months, and then she was gone. Dana was in Baltimore when it happened. She went in for a routine colonoscopy and ended up being one of those who die from the procedure in the country each year. Richard called Thomas to tell him. "I didn't know Mom was in trouble until a few days ago, and then it was too late to save her." This was on a bitterly cold January morning. Then six months later, Liz fell in the kitchen and fractured her hip. She was ninety-three now and, after the surgery, gradually lost weight, and her health declined. Her will to live evaporated; she died the week before Christmas. "Why?" Thomas asked. "Why does death's hand continue to knock at *my* door?"

Thomas, now seventy-two, tried to spend more hours at the store, but his heart wasn't in it. George and Mary called once a week from Arizona, where they now spent their winters, offering support and encouragement. Only they and Miff and Josie knew how emotionally drained Thomas had become. There are only so many times you can rebound, and with age, the energy and the will to do so weaken.

Mary was the one who came up with the idea: "Thomas needs a dog, George. Let's get one for him." Several months after Liz's death, a van pulled up to Thomas's shop, and Molly was delivered. For each, it was love at first sight. A note was attached to her collar: "A man's best friend through good times and bad. We love you, Thomas. Mary & George." Thomas framed the note and wrote the date on the back of the frame: January 22, 1992.

Two years later, Thomas turned seventy-five and turned the store over to Miff. Thomas didn't retire officially; he just came in when the spirit moved him.

Josie and Miff kept an eye on Thomas, but he was astonishingly self-reliant, maintaining muscle tone and flexibility with regular workouts at the Central School gym as well as being able to come up with a variety of tasty meals, whether he was cooking for himself or guests, a talent he had learned from Liz and Dana.

His routine held until Miff and Josie decided to move away. Dixville Crossing held too many memories of Cody, memories that refused to fade. After poring over maps and talking to friends, including George and Mary, whom they visited in Arizona, they decided on the Southwest, where Miff could fly year-round as a pilot for hire, and they could get away from the long, hard winters. They tried to convince Thomas to come with them, but he said he wouldn't leave the mountains he loved. The furniture store was closed, and Dixville Crossing lost its most successful enterprise. Elmo threw a town shindig at his bar and grill to celebrate the long run. Thomas and Miff were toasted frequently, and, of course, Lisette received her share of toasts, several of which brought the house down and even smiles from Miff. Finally, there was a send-off for Miff and Josie in the church annex. When they left, Thomas hunkered down to a daily routine of walking into town with Molly early in the morning, enjoying breakfast with the morning paper or a friend at the diner. The waitresses had taken to calling him the Philosopher. Then Molly would lead Thomas home, where he would clear his mind and meditate for an hour. Now that he was retired and had the time, he could free his mind of all thoughts, aided by the soft sound of the brook below the house. After meditating, Thomas would do odd chores until noon, followed by a workout. A light lunch preceded an afternoon nap; Molly curled up at his feet. Then, if weather permitted, he and Molly would take a walk. Tea would always follow, while listening to the news on public radio. As evening approached, Thomas would prepare one of his culinary creations, unless he had been invited out, and end his day reading or watching a little television before retiring. He followed events in Iraq with dismay and then alarm as the situation deteriorated, and he continued to struggle with the elusiveness of answers to the spiritual questions he so wished to resolve before he died. And Thomas kept coming back to those three words—*evolution*, *religion*, and *war*—how they interrelated, and the dissension and devastation caused by those words throughout recorded history.

Thomas rested his forehead in his hands on the back of the pew in front of him in hopes of clearing his head. When he looked up again at the altar, He was no longer there, and Molly was back at his feet between the pews. Another figure had taken His place, where He had been, dressed in elegant red vestments with an embroidered red cap. Thomas rubbed his eyes, but his blurred vision was only marginally improved. This figure too had a beard, but well trimmed and—

"Oh my God, it's you, the cardinal, the grand inquisitor," blurted Thomas.

"Quite so. Quite so," the cardinal replied with a strong Castilian accent.

"But where has He gone?"

"Him? The same place He went to when He left me in the dungeon, I imagine."

"And you?"

"Me? Oh, I have come to hear you out. He had heard enough."

"Hear me out?"

"Yes, the end of this modern version of my monologue to Him in Seville. Let's see, that's over five hundred years ago. I must say, my words have held up very well, very well indeed, wouldn't you agree, Thomas?"

Thomas exhaled a deep sigh and shook his head in disbelief. "I have nothing to say to you."

"Oh, come, come, Thomas. I've heard everything so far. Of course, I haven't been here in the church, but I have been within hearing range."

Thomas thought for a minute, recovering from his surprise and disappointment. "You are mocking me," he said.

"Mocking you? No, Thomas, I'm deadly serious."

"What a depressing thought."

"Now, now, we may not be as far apart as you think, Thomas."

"Hardly. I am a far cry from being a mass murderer."

"True, Thomas, and even though you are a well-meaning soul, had you come before me in Seville, I would have declared you too a heretic. You know, our only difference is my commitment to save mankind, albeit by deception. Better they have peace and their faith than know the truth and foul the earth more than it is already fouled."

"But you see," Thomas replied, "You lack any sense of compassion. I say to you there is another way, a way without your lavish robes of deceit. In Thomas's gospel omitted by the church founders from the New Testament—forsaking the church structure entirely—Christians believed they could and should spiritually commune directly with God, as sages and prophets did in the millennium prior to the Common Era. Or look at it this way, if one erases every thought from one's mind, there is left a void, and with that void comes an inner peace. This is a pure state; one might even say a godly state. Unfortunately, only a few *Homo sapiens* throughout history have learned how to combine this pure state of mind with an effective, compassionate, ethical code of conduct. And too often, those few are persecuted or murdered."

"A pure state? A godly state?" And the cardinal's chilling, triumphant smile told all. "Ah, how naive you are, Thomas."

Thomas continued. "Again, the word *evolution* seems apt here: not the physical aspects, which are so stressed and discussed but rather *Homo sapiens'* unfolding spirituality. Dinosaurs dominated the planet at one point because of their physical prowess. For the last few million years, *Homo sapiens* has dominated because of its cranial attributes. However, *Homo sapiens* has its Achilles' heel in that this cranial capacity has not developed in a uniform fashion. By that I simply mean tribalism, initially only communal, exists now on a global basis either by nationalism, religious differences, racial hatred, or in combination. As I speak, dozens of conflicts are in progress around the world in efforts to resolve differences between peoples. In many such conflicts over the centuries, millions have been killed, innocent victims of causes they would have fled from if they could."

"Of course, of course, for I have gained the upper hand," the cardinal interrupted.

"Nonsense," replied Thomas. "I am just telling you how events unfolded, events you had no part of. So let me continue."

The cardinal appeared impatient to change the subject but waved his hands saying, "Get on with it, then."

"Thank you," Thomas said. "You see, *Homo sapiens* has overpopulated parts of the world at the expense of other species. The unfortunate result, as witnessed in the last few hundred years and at an accelerating pace, is the inexorable desecration of the planet. In fact, *Homo sapiens* is now his own worst enemy. Many would argue the tipping point has passed. Is it not just a matter of time, with the cultural polarization of so many, combined with the increasing power of briefcase-sized weapons of mass destruction, when a few zealots or madmen with their own agendas will be in a position to bring the civilized world, warts and all, to its knees?"

"It will happen just as you say if I have anything to do with it," the cardinal said, as if it were a fait accompli.

"You'll have nothing to do with what happens. Our future rests with ourselves, which brings me to the role of religion in the scheme of things. Have not religions, over the last two thousand years, actually retarded *Homo sapiens*' spiritual development? As *Homo sapiens*' knowledge of the world around him expanded steadily from the dawn of the Renaissance to the present day, religion has been unable to adjust to a more informed intelligence. The result has been the marginalization, if not diminution of religions' influence and power.

"For instance, your church arguably reached its zenith of secular power and influence during the High Renaissance, but today it is simply a symbolic player on the world scene, having lost its leadership role in global affairs. Rather, it is more focused on addressing internal issues such as the need for celibacy, a woman's right to priesthood, child molestation cases, and pervasive homosexuality. Where it does engage in global issues, its position is often off the mark. Haven't you noticed? It has become a secular world dominated by generals, politicians, despots, and the like.

"The extraordinary range of *Homo sapiens*' knowledge today is remarkable. For instance, many still believe earthquakes, hurricanes, tsunamis, and the like are events brought about by the wrath of a god or gods. Two thousand years ago, the world was thought to be flat. Today we know that it is not only round but is a molten ball of fire with a thin crust, pieces of which slide around, slipping over and under one another, as geophysical pressures build and release, causing various degrees of chaos on the surface for its occupants. Hurricanes and typhoons unfold because of atmospheric disturbances and oceanic, seasonal variations. Droughts, floods, unexpected sudden climate changes, and the occasional asteroid hit from outer space cause similar chaotic events for all species.

"Knowing these facts, how does your church reconcile the massive suffering and deaths that occur? It used to be that God was punishing His living creatures for misdeeds of one kind or another, leaving it to them to figure it out. Today, the standard church rationale is that we do not know the answers, but God in his ultimate wisdom has His reasons, reasons we are not to question.

"So tell me, why would God create this topsy-turvy environment, and in six days, no less, according to His book? Our ever-expanding scientific explanations for how the planet and, for that matter, how the universe came to be, make infinitely more sense."

"Scientists never get it right. They are always correcting themselves," the cardinal said with disdain.

"The world is still round, is it not? And the earth revolves around the sun?"

"All right, all right, occasionally they're right."

"True, we do not have all of the answers, and maybe we never will, but there are sufficient pieces of the puzzle in place to make some solid observations, observations that are constantly being modified when new evidence is persuasive. So why, I would ask again, would God want to undercut the knowledge that man, in fits and starts, is systematically building and accumulating through the intellectual ability He gave to him? Answer me that. Just answer me that!"

"You say there are sufficient pieces of the puzzle in place to make some observations. For instance?"

"Well, we know that our universe—I say our universe since there may be others—is about thirteen or fourteen billion years old. The earth is some four billion years old. Primitive forms of life began in the oceans roughly four hundred million years ago, then aquatic life adapted to land. Dinosaurs held sway until most likely an asteroid collided with the planet approximately sixty million years ago, wiping out those beasts and others, severely changing the world climate and altering evolutionary patterns. What is at odds with a divine-being creation is that without this chance collision, apes and *Homo sapiens* most likely would never have evolved. Or are you going to tell me God hurled an asteroid to get rid of the dinosaurs so he could start creation all over with Adam?"

"See, that's just what I mean," the cardinal cried, pointing his finger at Thomas. "Every point you make has a qualifier: 'about,' 'roughly,' 'approximately,' 'most likely.' You expect me to take you seriously?"

"Please, let me finish my train of thought," Thomas replied.

"Must you?"

"Yes. When *Homo sapiens* does appear on the scene, having left the trees as apes to become bipedal and then migrating throughout the world, it takes some four and a half million years—and please don't nickel-and-dime me with the timeline here—before God makes His presence known through an insignificant nomadic Mediterranean tribe, the Hebrews. Are we to believe it took God ten billion years before it occurred to Him to create life? And then another four billion years before He made His presence known to a chosen handful?

"How different the world might be today if God had appeared *before Homo sapiens* began migrating throughout the world. Again, is not this sequence of events at odds with how a divine being would reveal himself to all of life? Let me ask you this: who's to say if God has revealed Himself, say, to elephants, whales, dolphins, cats, dogs, or *any* of the billions of life forms that exist on earth?

"Ah, but of course, we are the only life form to have a soul and are made in the image of God. How self-serving for us to claim exclusivity on the soul! And while we are talking about the soul, where do we find it? It is not part of our anatomy. While common usage is to refer to someone as 'He's a good soul,' where do we find this essence? Do other creatures of God have souls? If not, I would like that explained to me. At the moment of death, we refer to the soul or the spirit 'taking leave of the body.' Does this occur at the moment of death to all living creatures, or just *Homo sapiens*? Were creatures swimming, crawling, flying, and walking around for billions of years aimlessly with or without souls before God declared Himself? And if these essences did not exist prior to His declaring Himself, when were these essences received: at conception, at birth, or later? Or were souls an optional add-on to His creatures? Some got them. Some didn't. Tell me."

But as the cardinal started to respond, Thomas cut him off. "Let me offer another possibility: some might have been given flawed souls."

"Flawed souls?" the cardinal asked, suddenly curious.

"You are familiar with the term *human genome*?"

"Yes . . . I am aware of those words," the cardinal said with a certain lack of conviction. "Also known as the hereditary code of life, I believe?"

"You surprise me, being so au courant. I can be succinct then."

"I am always being underestimated," the cardinal murmured to himself.

"Well, this code of life is carried in each cell of *Homo sapiens* consisting of six billion units, yes, that's six *billion*. Three billion units are passed from each parent to their newborn. Of this total, every offspring randomly receives a small number of new units or mutations, mutations that may either be beneficial, of no consequence, or harmful. In other words, every life form is born with a flawed hereditary code with mutations that can result in diseases or birth defects.

"The obvious question then is: Would a divine being create an imperfect hereditary code for his living creatures at the time of their conception when just a handful of the six billion units may doom one or more of the succeeding offspring at birth? Isn't this at odds with a divine being? Is a soul, possibly an imperfect one, wrapped up in one or more of these microscopic units?

"I have acknowledged that there are answers we do not have and maybe never will, but we are continually modifying observations when new evidence is compelling. So why, I ask again, would God want to undercut the knowledge that *Homo sapiens* is systematically accumulating? Answer me that. I ask you again, to answer this question."

"Well done, Thomas, well done!" The cardinal gently clapped his hands together several times. "Are you finished now?"

"Nearly." But as Thomas spoke, he felt his strength and his resolve slipping away from him. The cardinal had been shifting in and out of focus as he had spoken. Thomas was noticeably perspiring now, and the numbness on his right side was more pronounced, particularly his right arm, which now hung limply at his side, devoid of feeling. Too, his words were becoming more difficult to form and, when uttered, were slurring more. "I will be brief," Thomas added as he pushed himself back in the pew with his left hand and leaned against the pew divider.

"You, an admitted nonbeliever, an atheist, believe that only through His church and belief in the Holy Trinity can social and spiritual order be maintained in the world. Without this faith, the world would dissolve in chaos. So the deceit has to be perpetuated at all costs, even if it means burning thousands upon thousands of innocents at the stake.

"I, on the other hand, think of myself as an enlightened transcendentalist. By that I mean I do not acknowledge the existence of a supreme being in the sense in which your church does. Rather, I accept there to be simply the unknowable, which is presently beyond the grasp of *Homo sapiens*. History records spiritual beliefs through the ages that run the gamut, and there is no sign yet that this pattern will disappear. If these beliefs gather enough momentum at the same time and bump into one another as they invariably do, conflicts result. I rest my case with Christianity and Islam today. Look at where the Hebrew concept of God has led us.

"Initially, their god, Yahweh, was seen as a charismatic, often vengeful, warrior god who personally involved himself on earth with certain Hebrew followers in the manner of the Hellenistic, Homeric tradition. But as Yahweh matured, He took on a more transcendent and distant persona removed from his earlier earthly visits or involvements. Then, with the coming of Christ, a cataclysmic clash occurred. The Hebrew prophets had been heralding the coming of their god as a king descending from the heavens in all his glory, announcing the Day of Judgment, and on that occasion, all earthly wrongs and inequities would be set right. Moreover, the expectation was that His arrival would be soon.

"Jesus, as we know, fell far short of these expectations—so much so that the Hebrews believed Him to be only another prophet and not the Son of God, as His disciples and followers maintained. After Christ's Crucifixion, His disciples announced Jesus's deified death, as three days later, He rose from the dead, visiting some of them before joining His Father in the kingdom of heaven, if we believe their account.

"Those who believed that Jesus was the Son of God broke ranks with the Hebrews to become known as Christians. Gradually, the Christians gained the upper hand, and although they were a splintered group, one group declaring the other heretical, the Hebrews became marginalized, persecuted, and, in a sense, left out in the cold, feeling that somehow their religion had been hijacked and then reinvented by the Christians. Christians, however, were not only involved in infighting but were also persecuted by the Romans until Constantine came to their rescue.

"But another Christian issue remained unresolved: the nature of Jesus's divinity. The solution? God was to become the first person of a Trinity consisting of His Son, Jesus, and an entity to be known as the Holy Spirit. Once this unique and complex spiritual integration was complete, the next two thousand years pass as if God, His Son, and the Holy Spirit had left town.

"On the other hand, Muslims maintain that at the turn of the seventh century, God makes his presence known again, as Allah, and speaks to the prophet Muhammad, whereupon Allah's words are written down creating the holy book, the Qur'an. Since God's most recent appearance was to the Muslims, it is they who claim to 'have it right.'

"So now we have three holy books: the Tanakh texts, the Holy Bible, and the Qur'an, with three differing deities. Yahweh; God the Father, Son, and Holy Spirit, or Trinity; and Allah."

The cardinal waved his hand. "Deceits, Thomas, all deceits."

"Ah," Thomas replied, "but the point I wish to make is that *Homo sapiens* does not need deceits in this day and age to satisfy his thirst for transcendence. It is laughable, really, that Allah and God the Father, Son, and Holy Spirit now are fighting themselves: the Qur'an versus the Holy Bible, Muslim against Christian. Perhaps the Tanakh's Yahweh is the referee?"

"And Satan smiles!" injected the cardinal again.

"Master of Deceits, I am emboldened to ask you a question. Disguised, as we speak, as the infamous cardinal, aren't you, how shall I say this gracefully, but an invented New Testament figure, introduced by the gospel writers to provide the rationale for a cosmic struggle between good and evil for which Christ died?"

The cardinal straightened in the altar chair, his eyes piercing Thomas. Taken by surprise by the old man's last words, he said nothing, so Thomas continued. "Now, I'd like to expose you for who you really are. Initially, you are introduced to us by Isaiah in the Old Testament as an insignificant fallen angel, who then comes to act as a messenger for God, testing the beliefs of his chosen people, a mere gofer doing God's dirty work. Balaam is so tested by you in the book of Numbers, Job in the book of Job. But when God sends his Son to minister unto His people, the eventual New Testament gospel writers realize there is a problem. In the book of Genesis, Adam is told by God not to eat from the fruit of the tree in paradise or he will die. The serpent then tells Eve to eat the fruit as it will not bring death but rather they will be like God, knowing both good and evil. Adam and Eve eat the fruit, and God curses the serpent, whom He identifies as a 'devil.' Then, once they disobey Him, He does not kill them but drives them out of paradise. Here, at the very beginning of time, according to the holy book, God is forbidding use of the inquiring mind He created. Rather, a devil in the form of a serpent overrides God's command. And what is a devil doing in paradise in the first place?"

The cardinal rose from his chair to speak, but again Thomas waved him down. "Please."

The cardinal sat down.

"The way I see it, without the serpent, a devil, an adversary, there is no story. After the creation, mankind lives forever in paradise? No, that does not jibe with the world in which the Old Testament books were written. Surrounding the Kingdom of Israel, nations were warring; the world was a cruel and hostile place. The Old Testament writers were looking for their God to come and set things right. Over time, the serpent in paradise morphs into a fallen angel from heaven, to a gofer for God, and finally to God's equal from the dark side: Satan, ruler of hell. But the turning point comes when God sends His Son to us. His brief ministry is so controversial, so bewildering that unless an adversary is woven into the fabric of His life, there exists no explanation as to why God sent Him in the first place. How can Christ die for our sins if evil does not exist, if there is not an Antichrist to be defeated? God in heaven. Satan in hell. The four gospel writers of the New Testament all address this confrontation. Satan tempts Christ in the wilderness. Judas, or is it the Master of Deceits, betrays Christ? The multitude picks Barabbas, a condemned thief, surely Satan's agent, to be freed, sending Jesus to be crucified? The Day of Judgment was expected while Christ's disciples were still living, or did Satan prevent that from happening?

"And where are we twenty-one hundred years later? The United States, undisputed leader of the free world, designates Iraq, Iran, and North Korea as an 'axis of evil' for their sponsorship of various terrorist cells now collectively referred to as al Qaeda. The former, in turn, is viewed as the Great Satan by this axis and many other countries. You've even made it to the United Nations, according to Hugo Chávez, president of Venezuela, who said of our country's president George Bush's appearance the day before: 'The devil came here yesterday, right here. It smells of sulfur still today, this table that I am now standing in front of.' I suspect more people took Chávez seriously than laughed at those words."

"You see, I have made inroads, great inroads," the cardinal broke in. "The world is topsy-turvy. And my work is not done. What is to stop me?"

"Not religion," Thomas offered.

"Then is there anything?" pressed the cardinal. "Answer me."

"That is the question, for the world is in free fall and your stock is looking 'good'—forgive me, but I couldn't resist. But if this descent is to be reversed, everyone must accept the view that we are one family, to be sure a very large one, who live in a house known as planet Earth. And in order to live together under one roof, there cannot be unruly members. Differences, yes, within guidelines, are accepted and encouraged, including spiritual orientations. But looking to the heavens for approval to justify one's actions usurps individual responsibilities members must have for one another, as well as the resolve to come to terms with these differences peacefully in a civilized way. Religions have not proven to be the answer. In fact, I would argue religions have muzzled spirituality, wrapped and suffocated it in dogmas. Our lives are too short—we all die—too filled with suffering beyond our control, facing too many challenges, and presented with too many opportunities to better the world to squander them on intransigent religious points of view and conflicts. Would Christians be so gripped by their religion if Saint Peter's pearly gates did not await them or Muslims by Islam if seventy-two vestal virgins did not await the men? Rather, what if at an early age, children were exposed to the myriad of fascinating and exciting ways their spiritual being can be developed as they grow into adults, and they were allowed to choose over time the flavor or flavors they felt most comfortable with, subject to modification, even change over time?"

"But there's the rub," the cardinal interrupted. "A universally accepted code of conduct? That will never happen. Let me explain something to you. Homo sapiens, *at the moment anyway, is the species atop the food chain, as other species have been before it. And like its predecessors, a given species evolves not only in relation to others but also at the expense of its own kind in attempts to assure its dominance and survival. Darwin demonstrated this by his evolutionary discoveries on the Galápagos Islands. The name of the game is survival, plain and simple. The weapons are primarily twofold: reproductive fecundity and establishing and maintaining the highest possible rung on the food chain by any means. The common method is to kill and eat species beneath you or weaker individuals of your own kind. For instance, if the food chain for one species becomes unavailable or the climate changes as to be unlivable, the species must evolve quickly enough to adapt to other sources or climates, or die off.*

"Today, Homo sapiens *populations continue to grow in frightening numbers, causing massive disruption of the planet's food chain with no signs of reaching a reproductive equilibrium and balance in relation to other life forms.* Homo sapiens *is no different from most other species: men*

are hunters and gatherers, territorial, greedy, rarely bonding outside their own kind within the species and instinctively reproducing to perpetuate themselves. All of these characteristics are embedded in what now is known as one's DNA. So you see, old man, the devil is in the DNA details, and these details are stronger than any universal code of conduct. You need only observe the gradual, and now likely irreversible, acceleration of the global ecosystem collapse before your very eyes while you vainly reach toward the heavens to be saved."

"You may be right on that. I must confess *Homo sapiens* has failed to learn from his mistakes. Over and over, history repeats itself, and as the planet shrinks, *Homo sapiens* becomes increasingly polarized and intransigent regarding issues confronting everyone and everything. The troublemakers, formerly empires, are now competing countries, rogue or failed states, and terrorist cells with the prospect in a few years of one madman holding the world hostage. On this track, what chance does a universal code of conduct have? His Grace has left us as mysteriously as He came, and I find myself in the end agreeing with you."

As the cardinal appeared to consider this, Thomas felt such a shortness of breath, he gasped for air. The cardinal now seemed to be rising from his chair and to be floating, his robe gently swaying. Suddenly Thomas buckled and, with a soft groan, slipped to the floor. As he lay there, life having left him, Molly's warm tongue licked his mouth—a kiss of love, quite unlike the kiss Christ gave the "bloodless aged lips" of Dostoevsky's grand inquisitor.

The first few parishioners who entered the First Congregational Church did not notice Thomas or Molly, who remained at his side. Rob and Mary Townsend were the first to see them lying between two pews, and quickly Thomas was raised and carried out into the annex, with Molly whimpering as she followed.

No more than two dozen people attended the Sunday service that day, briefly delayed by Thomas's death. "A good soul," intoned Pastor Harden to the congregation, "a thoughtful man with an inquiring mind, who experienced more than his share of grief and sadness, and who wrestled with the meaning of life. God will receive him kindly. Now he will have peace." Several parishioners added expressions of sympathy. A few days later, Thomas was cremated. The following summer, his ashes were spread on Pilgrim Mountain by Miff and Josie and George and Mary. Molly was adopted by the Clarksons, but she never bonded with them as she had with Thomas. The following year, to the surprise of both Miff and Josie, Josie became pregnant.

One lingering mystery remained. Pastor Harden could not recall lighting the candles on the communion table that morning, although he had arrived early at the rector's study to put the final touches on his sermon. "A senior moment," he surmised.

★★★

"So, Alyosha, what do you think of this senseless poem, more nonsense from your brother, who remains an unrepentant student after all these years?"

"Ivan, such modesty is unbecoming," Alyosha exclaimed.

"You like it, then?"

"Your long-suffering doubting Thomas, by freeing his spiritual being from what he comes to see as the constraint of traditional religion, achieves an enlightened transcendence of his own making."

"You have been listening, Alyosha. However, do I sense a shift perhaps in your long-held Christian beliefs?"

Alyosha paused.

"Come, come, now. No secrets between us."

"Then I shall tell you something I've told no one."

"What's this? Something you've kept from me?"

"Yes, Ivan, this is true. Hear me out. Some years ago, I journeyed to Basel to see the painting for myself."

"You what?"

"You heard me, Ivan."

"And? Alyosha, what did you think? Why haven't you told me? When did you make this journey?"

"Ivan, quiet and let me tell you. No more questions now until I've finished."

Ivan raised his hands. "Forgive me. Do continue."

"When did I make the journey? Many years ago, actually. It makes no difference. Perhaps a decade after you went and saw the painting. I do remember it was in the fall. Switzerland is beautiful then. Remember how, when you returned to Russia after seeing it, you couldn't stop talking about it? I can hear you now. 'Alyosha! You must go to Basel. There is this extraordinary painting by Hans Holbein the Younger in the museum there of the dead Christ. It is called the Body of the Dead Christ in the

Tomb. *You see, Holbein has painted a dead Jew who has just been crucified, taken down from the cross, and stretched out, appearing to be no more than a bloody mortal corpse. Holbein's figure is Christ only by the title of the painting, not by whom you see in the painting.' And then I came to make the journey to Basel and viewed the painting. I felt as if my faith had been pierced to its core. You never spoke of the painting's size, some six feet long and less than a foot high, Ivan. The figure is doubly entombed: both by the painted tomb and by the picture frame. There is no, nor can there be any, escape! Ever since, Ivan, I ask myself: what if Christ was simply a prophet, as the Jews believe, just a human being like you and me? Your senseless poem, as you call it, Ivan, is a Holbein poem!"*

"Let me put it to you this way, Alyosha. Does not Christ appear more entombed to you now, if that is possible, than when you first viewed Him?"

"Oh, Ivan, I do wish you hadn't asked me that," replied Alyosha with a sigh.

"But I have asked you," pressed Ivan.

"It pains me deeply," Alyosha said softly, "to have to say yes, for faith holds less meaning in the secular world of today, Ivan, where men believe their destiny rests in their own hands. Where has faith led man over the last three millennia? I must say, Thomas's points are well taken. Faith in what? The institution of the Catholic Church? Yahweh, God, or Allah suddenly appearing to take believers to heaven and banish the rest to eternal damnation? Is this how we go forward in our longing for spiritual nourishment?"

"Ah, what you have just said reminds me of that nineteenth-century Palmyra prophet who also believed Judgment Day was imminent—and would take place in Independence, Missouri, in America, no less, at which

time his followers there would be swept up to heaven. You know about the Palmyra prophet, Alyosha?"

"You mean Joseph Smith?" Alyosha replied.

"I do. And what do you make of this American prophet, who through revelations had described in great detail the heaven of God awaiting his followers? Does Smith's Book of Mormon supersede Muhammad's Qur'an? Does the Qur'an then supersede the Holy Bible, which, of course, must supersede the Tanakh, if we are to believe the followers of each succeeding religion? Is it not all a matter of faith and how one is raised, predispositions which unfold growing up, and influences of others determining spiritual orientation or lack thereof?

"Let us take a closer look at the Palmyra prophet. At age eighteen, a poor uneducated farm boy says an angel, Moroni, visits him one night in his bedroom, standing above the floor in a brilliant shaft of white light, and proceeds to tell him about a book written on gold plates buried on a nearby hill. With the plates, the angel confides, are two stone crystals fastened to a breastplate—the Urim and Thummim—interpreters for translating the book, since the characters on the plates are Egyptian hieroglyphics. A subsequent vision tells Smith precisely where on the hill to look for the book. Once the plates have been retrieved, Smith translates them covered in cloth on a table, not using the Urim and Thummim interpreters provided, but by using his own seer stone placed in an inverted black hat into which Smith peers without ever looking at the plates themselves. Purportedly, the 584-page Book of Mormon is written from this visionary translation—only a few hundred miles west of the Adirondacks, I might add.

"The life of the Palmyra prophet is a tumultuous one. Smith is bombarded with revelations from God over a twenty-year period, including one blessing plural marriages. He and his followers are driven from one town to another.

Then, at age thirty-eight, while he is in jail awaiting trial on charges of treason, a mob breaks in and shoots him. Yet enough Mormons stayed the course during Smith's lifetime to carry the faith forward. Today, less than two hundred years later, there are six million believers in America and another six and a half million worldwide."

"And you view Mormonism as a legitimate Christian spin-off then, Ivan?"

"Absolutely. But more important, Alyosha, to what extent are other religions challenged, even undermined, by Smith's revelations? What combination of factors gave Smith enough traction to be accepted today as an authentic prophet by twelve and a half million people? What I am saying is that there are undeniable similarities between Smith, Muhammad, and Christ."

"You can't be serious in comparing the three?"

"Well, all three had no formal education and first appealed mainly to the poor and uneducated. All three were persecuted. All three communicated directly with God and acted as revelators to their followers. All three were charismatic. All three were associated with miracles, although Christ certainly stood far above the others in this regard. Each commanded authority over his believers—certainly Muhammad's strong suit. His profile is not unlike Constantine's. And finally, there is a certain amount of mystery that surrounds each one. Smith is certainly the most challenging to come to terms with. Christ's great mystery, of course, is whether he was a prophet like the other two or was in fact the Son of God. In short, the basic ingredients—charisma, miracles, authority, and mystery—must all be present for a prophet to gain a following in sufficient numbers for the term 'religion' to be applied. With that said, believers must have faith in the revelations of the prophet. Without faith, the prophet is viewed as a charlatan. His followers must believe that their prophet has a direct communication with God. And faith is very fickle, present one day, gone the next."

"This implies that the spiritual needs of the followers require continual scriptual nourishment," Alyosha added.

"Exactly."

Alyosha paused for a moment, and Ivan noted sadness in his eyes. Then Alyosha continued. "Let me put it this way: man needs to stop looking to the heavens and get a grip on the mess he alone has created before it is too late."

"And in so doing, develop an outreach of personal fellowship," Ivan interjected.

"Ah," Alyosha replied. "I like that phrase. It has a global ring to it. But you, dear brother, I see you have mellowed over the years. You are not the uncompromising atheist now, are you?"

"The world has changed, Alyosha, and look at how much more we know about it—not that it does us a bit of good. We have come from the age of Constantine, where Christianity became an essential factor in strengthening the Roman Empire, to an age where not only Christianity but also religions generally are under increasing pressure. If we accept our world fast becoming a global village, then we are back to where the Roman Empire was with a mix of religions under one roof. However improbable, we would be better off than we are now, would we not, blending them together into one hybrid religion under one deity? Otherwise, religions will continue to compete for souls, endlessly challenging one another while fading into the sunset.

"I'd only add that if we are going to be judged in the hereafter, we will surely be judged on how we led our lives, whether clothed in religious dogma or not. The grand inquisitor believed that without His church, the world would collapse into chaos. His error was in believing his or any religion could save humanity. As we now see, religion appears to be having the opposite effect, actually inciting global chaos."

"But I have one question for you, Ivan."

"And that is?"

"Your formula 'everything is lawful': will you still not renounce it, and with it the Karamazov baseness?"

"Ah, Alyosha, I should have known you would ask me that again. I was but a youth then, living under the skirts of Mother Russia. Now I am older, but still young by biblical standards, mind you. But while the world is fast becoming a global village, Mother Russia, fragmented, corrupt, and poor except for the oligarchs and bureaucrats, is no longer invincible. As for the Karamazov baseness, that is history. But no, I still will not renounce my 'everything is lawful' formula, Alyosha. Mother Russia hasn't, and if nothing else, I am still Russian.

"Alas, the real tragedy lies in the fact that now religious leaders have co-opted the 'everything-is-lawful-if-you-don't-convert' label to justify acts of atrocity, acts by Muslims in the name of Allah, acts by Christians in the name of theocratic democracy, disparate cultures facing off against one another. And you and I were led to believe that the salvation of the world lay with Christianity eventually prevailing as the only religion on the planet. That hope, Alyosha, appears to have all but evaporated in the span of a mere two generations. No, if a civilized global village is in the process of unfolding, leaders with common sets of ethical principles, principles universally taught, accepted, and applied must prevail. Time is running out, if it has not run out already."

As he had before, Alyosha went to his brother and kissed him on the lips. "I like doubting Thomas as your twenty-first-century inquisitor, Ivan. He has values and is compassionate. You have given him . . ." Alyosha paused.

"Sensibility and sensitivity," Ivan added.

"Amen."

"Alyosha, it is time we part."

"And will you promise me another such poem in the years ahead?"

Ivan thought for a moment. "No promises this time, Alyosha, no promises." And with that, Ivan returned his brother's kiss and took his leave.

Author's Note

For further reading and/or viewing, the reader may find the books and films listed below of interest.

Armstrong, Karen. *The Great Transformation: The Beginning of Our Religious Traditions*. New York: Alfred A. Knopf, 2006.

Baigent, Michael, Richard Leigh, and Henry Lincoln. *The Holy Blood and the Holy Grail*. London: Arrow Books, 1996.

Bartley, M. *Grisha: The Story of Cellist Gregor Piatigorsky*. New Russia, N.Y.: Otis Mountain Press, 2004.

Belloc, Hilaire. *The Great Heresies*. Rockford, Ill.: Tan Books and Publishers, Inc., 1991.

Bernard, Dr. R. W. *Apollonious of Tyana the Nazarene.* Sacramento: Ancient Wisdom Publications, 2010.

Bloom, Harold. *Jesus and Yahweh: The Names Divine*. New York: Riverhead Books, Published by the Penguin Group, 2005.

Brown, Dan. *Angels and Demons*. New York: Pocket Books, 2000.

Brown, Dan. *The Da Vinci Code*. New York: Doubleday, 2003.

Carroll, James. *Constantine's Sword: The Church and the Jews; A History.* New York: Houghton Mifflin Company, 2001.

Collins, Francis S. *The Language of God*. New York: Free Press, 2006.

Dalton, Dennis G. *Power over People; Philosophy & Intellectual History; Lecture Thirteen: Dostoevsky's Grand Inquisitor: 'The Great Courses'*. Chantilly, Va.: The Teaching Company Limited Partnership, 1991.

Dawkins, Richard. *The God Delusion*. Great Britain: Bantam Books, 2006.

Dennett, Daniel C. *Breaking the Spell: Religion as a Natural Phenomenon*. New York: Viking, Published by the Penguin Group, 2006.

Dever, William G. *What Did the Biblical Writers Know and When Did They Know It? What Archaeology Can Tell Us about the Reality of Ancient Israel*. Grand Rapids, Mich.: William B. Eerdmans Publishing C., 2001.

Dostoevsky, Fyodor. *The Brothers Karamazov*. Translated by Andrew R. MacAndrew, introductory essay by Konstantin Mochulski, New York: A Bantam Book, 1970.

Dostoevsky, Fyodor. *The Grand Inquisitor: With Related Chapters from The Brothers Karamazov*. Edited and introduced by Charles B. Guignon, translated by Constance Garnett. Indianapolis: Hackett Publishing Company, 1993.

Dostoevsky, Fyodor. *The Grand Inquisitor.* Introduction by Anne Fremantle. New York: Continuum International Publishing Group, 2005.

Dostoevsky, Fyodor. *Notes from the Underground and The Grand Inquisitor with Relevant Works by Chernyshevsky, Shchedrin and Dostoevsky*. Selection, translation and introduction by Ralph E. Matlaw. New York: E. P. Dutton & Co., Inc., 1960.

Ehrman, Bart D. *Lost Christianities: Christian Scriptures and the Battles over Authentication, "The Great Courses"*. Chantilly, Va.: The Teaching Company Limited Partnership, 2002.

Ehrman, Bart D. *Truth and Fiction in the Da Vinci Code*. New York: Oxford University Press, 2004.

Fox, Robin Lane. *Pagans and Christians*. New York: Alfred A. Knopf, Inc., 1989.

Frank, Joseph. *Dostoevsky: A Writer in His Time*. Princeton, N.J.: Princeton University Press, 2010.

Frazer, James George. *The Golden Bough: A Study in Magic and Religion*. New York: A Touchstone Book, Published by Simon & Schuster, 1996.

Funk, Robert W., and the Jesus Seminar. *The Search for the Authentic Deeds of Jesus*. New York: A Polebridge Press Book, Harper Collins, 1998.

Funk, Robert W., and the Jesus Seminar. *The Search for the Authentic Words of Jesus*. New York: Harper Collins, 1997.

Gibbon, Edward. *The Decline and Fall of the Roman Empire*. New York: The Heritage Press, 1946.

Gibran, Kahlil. *The Prophet*. N.Y.: Alfred A. Knopf, MCMXXVIII

Harris, Sam. *The End of Faith: Religion, Terror and the Future of Reason*. New York: W. W. Norton & Company, 2004.

Hirsi Ali, Ayaan. *Infidel*. New York: Free Press, 2007.

Holy Bible. Authorized King James Version. Edinburgh: William Collins, Sons and Company, Limited, 1943.

Hitchens, Christopher. *God Is Not Great: How Religion Poisons Everything.* New York: Twelve Hachette Book Group USA, 2007.

Huntington, Samuel P. *The Clash of Civilizations and Remaking of World Order* New York: Simon & Schuster Paperbacks, 1996.

Lewis, Bernard. *The Crisis of Islam*. New York: Modern Library, 2003.

Lewis, Bernard. *What Went Wrong*. New York: Oxford University Press, 2002.

Lunn, Martin. *Da Vinci Code Decoded*. New York: The Disinformation Company, Ltd., 2004.

Manchester, William. *A World Lit Only by Fire: The Medieval Mind and the Renaissance; Portrait of an Age*. Boston: Back Bay Books, Little, Brown and Company, 1992.

Mann, Brian. *Welcome to the Homeland*. Hanover, N.H.: Steerforth Press, 2006.

Menand, Louis. *The Metaphysical Club*. New York: Farrar, Straus & Giroux, 2001.

Pagels, Elaine. *Beyond Belief: The Secret Gospel of Thomas*. New York: Random House, 2005.

Pagels, Elaine. *The Gnostic Gospels*. New York: Random House, 1979.

Pagels, Elaine. *The Origin of Satan*. New York: Vintage Books, 1995.

Partner, Peter. *Two Thousand Years The First Millennium, The Birth of Christianity to the Crusades*. Foreword by Melvyn Bragg. London: Sevenoaks, 2002.

Pelikan, Jaroslav. *Whose Bible Is It? A History of the Scriptures through the Ages*. New York: Viking, Published by The Penguin Group, 2005.

Picknett, Lynn, and Clive Prince. *The Templar Revelation: Secret Guardians of the True Identity of Christ*. London: Corgi Books, 1998.

Pickthall, Mohammad M. *The Glorious Qur'an*. Des Plaines, Ill.: Published by Library of Islam, 1994.

Prothero, Stephen. *American Jesus: How the Son of God Became a National Icon*. New York: Farrar, Straus & Giroux, 2003.

Renan, Ernest. *The Life of Jesus*. New York: The Modern Library, 1927.

Salvini, Emil R. *Hobey Baker, American Legend*. Saint Paul, Minn.: The Hobey Baker Memorial Foundation, 2005.

Singh, Simon. *Big Bang: The Origin of the Universe*. New York: HarperCollins, 2004.

Smith, Huston. *The World's Religions: Our Great Wisdom Traditions*. New York: HarperCollins, 1991.

Steyn, Mark. *America Alone*. Washington, D.C.: Regnery Publishing, Inc., 2006.

Tyson, Neil deGrasse and Donald Goldsmith. *Origins: Fourteen Billion Years of Cosmic Evolution*. New York: W.W. Norton & Company, 2004.

Wells, Spencer. *The Journey of Man: A Genetic Odyssey*. New York: Random House, 2003.

Wills, Gary. *What Jesus Meant*. New York: Viking, Published by the Penguin Group, 2006.

Wright, Lawrence. *The Looming Tower*. New York: Alfred A. Knopf, Inc., 2006.

Wright, Robert. *The Evolution of God*. New York: Little Brown and Company, 2009.

Films

Elmer Gantry. MGM DVD Home Video. Director: Richard Brooks, 1960.

From Jesus to Christ: The First Christians. Frontline PBS/DVD Home Video. Director: William Cran, 2009.

Inherit the Wind. MGM/DVD Home Video. Starring Spencer Tracy, Frederic March, and Gene Kelly (1960 Feature Film). Metro-Goldwyn-Mayer Studios, 1960.

Jesus of Nazareth. MGM VHS Home Video. Director: Franco Zeffirelli, 1992.

Journey of Man: The Story of the Human Species. Hosted by Dr. Spencer Wells. PBS Home Video. Tigress Productions, 2003.

"Oh,God!" Warner Brothers VHS Home Video. Director Carl Reiner,1977.

Origins: Fourteen Billion Years of Cosmic Evolution. Hosted by author, Neil deGrasse Tyson. WGBH/BOSTON Video. NOVA, 2004.

The Brothers Karamazov. MGM/UA VHS Home Video. Starring Yul Brynner and Claire Bloom (1957 Feature Film) Turner Entertainment, 1957.

The Buddha: The Story of Siddhartha. PBS/DVD Home Video. Director: David Grubin, 2010.

The Longest Day. Twentieth Century Fox DVD Home Video. Director: Darryl F. Zanuck. Darryl F. Zanuck Productions, Inc. and Twentieth Century Fox Film Corporation, 1962.

What Darwin Never Knew. NOVA/PBS DVD Item No: 6188.

Made in the USA
Lexington, KY
19 December 2010